*After Armageddon?*

Science fiction is a literature of ideas. It is also a literature of adventure, quest, and speculation. In these days of the latter third of the Twentieth Century, it follows that its concepts often reflect that which is the concern of the time.

In TESTAMENT XXI we present the first novel of one of that generation which will determine the fate of the balance of this century. On the surface, it could be said that TESTAMENT XXI is another novel about the world after a devastating war—the underground city and the problems of its survivors.

But TESTAMENT XXI is much more than that. It is a novel of speculation and intent. Guy Snyder, its author, has used it as a vehicle to outline the kind of speculation which has been the province of such writers as Thomas M. Disch, Mark Geston, and Harlan Ellison. It may be read on whatever level you choose. *But on any level you will not want to miss a remarkable science fiction experience.*

# TESTAMENT XXI

by
Guy Snyder

DAW BOOKS, INC.

DONALD A. WOLLHEIM, PUBLISHER

1301 Avenue of the Americas
New York, N. Y.       10019

Published by
THE NEW AMERICAN LIBRARY
OF CANADA LIMITED

To Laura,
and the past
the present
perhaps
the future

First Printing, July, 1973

1 2 3 4 5 6 7 8 9

# PART 1

# Dreams

## I

There was a desert.

It really wasn't a desert, it was a wasteland, and not much of a wasteland.

The inhabitants of the area in need of a better locution called it a desert.

During the day buzzards flew about it. In the heat various small reptiles, a lot of them suggestive of weird mutations of the chameleon, slithered about on whatever God had given them in the form of primitive propulsion. Heat pointed up to the sky in the summer. Occasionally, a deer wandered about looking for a forest. The animals from the nearby, and sometimes normal, "good" country had a pronounced tendency to get lost in the desert, cut off from their groups. Eventually they died on the desert floor, the climate wouldn't tolerate them; it was—well, the climate wasn't hospitable for them. They died either of the local poisoning or thirst, depending on their individual capabilities. The buzzard, a very adaptable bird, eventually took care of the flesh.

The buzzards.

The buzzards were always rather thin.

The buzzards had a rather hard time of it. They are a most hated and yet a most necessary fowl. Sometimes, when the weather was in their favor, the buzzards would eat very well. They were not really native to this area—no man knew where they had come from. All of a sudden, they were just there, gliding along the air currents. Perhaps someone had forgotten to close a grave somewhere nearby, and they had ascended upward from Hell.

It got fairly hot at times on the desert floor in the summer, but rarely over one hundred degrees Fahrenheit.

The desert was a burned out area about fifty-two square miles in area.

During the winter, the desert got fairly cold. Not much grew on the ground. When rain or snow fell, the residue washed into a river that divided the area almost in half. The river was cutting a canyon. There was terrible soil erosion. The air could not be breathed for extended periods of time without modification—minutes were chances.

The desert, even when viewed from the comfort of an observation bubble, left one with a terrible sensation of nothing—an unwashed feeling of monotony.

The sky was the perpetual color of steel in a fire: intense and solid blue in the heat.

Occasionally, one would find the standing, or just fallen, ruin of a tree.

Trees were more common out from the center of the desert—heading toward the still grassed and forested "goodlands" that surrounded the area; but no land was good. Many of the trees were once well-grown. The ones still standing? The majority of them were oak, for their flesh didn't rot away too fast. Were they still alive? It seemed rather amazing that even oak would have stood for so long.

There was one nearby that was still alive. It was close to the river and its roots drank the flowing water. It grew leaves: odd, queer-shaped leaves. No acorns. It provided some shade for the twisted animals that were smart enough to get their water from places other than the river. Soon, the canyon-cutting stream would undermine the roots of the oak, and then that too would fall.

There were a lot of bones left on the desert and in the ruins, bleached white by the sun—very cleanly picked.

The nights were better. The stars would come out, and the sky turned a black onyx in coloration and was always extremely clear. There was normally nothing to spoil the view of the Milky Way.

On the desert floor a few trails still existed; they were best seen from the rare craft in flight. To the lizards that sunned themselves on the upturned chunks and rocks of pavement ripped up from the once flat roadbeds, they were quite natural formations.

Most of the lizards were about the size of a good Republic rat. Their skin was sandy brown in color, and had the texture of the pavement chunks. They blended well with the natural environment and had a tendency to overbreed. Some were developing a third, though blind, eye.

The superhighways were destroyed, twisted nightmares that had died of shock.

... I want no memories; no memories ...

There were some sparse grasslike plants here and there. No cactus, nothing like those put on the resource tapes for the bright children of the King and Queen and Church.

In the middle of virtually nowhere, a dandelion with a blossom three feet in diameter grew; it was always in bloom. It never went to seed. It was rather pretty.

rape
rape
rape

There was one road in good repair. It was on top of a twenty-foot high concrete mound, and it was an all black road in the shape of a circle seventy feet in diameter and fifteen feet wide. Within this road, there was a fifty by fifty-foot square made out of some metallic material, and this square could be lowered down into the earth, way below the level of the surface. A black bull's-eye was painted on it.

There were four shining archways set in the surface mound and, out about twenty feet from the sloped edge of the mound, there was a ground level observation bubble positioned on the side of a road that led into each archway from a second circle of pavement which surrounded the mound.

The outer circle of pavement was one hundred feet from the archways of the mound. From the archway heading east, the road was thirty feet wide and it did not stop at the outer pavement circle. It continued outward about one thousand yards past a very rusted outer parameter of barbed wire, and then crumbled to chunks and slabs a little way farther out. On the maps, the road eventually connected to Interstate 96, which for all practical purposes was a graveyard.

The observation posts were made of a special shielded glass that was a dull green in color. They rested on shiny, stainless steel bases. A rather short, dull black barrel projected out of each bubble. The entire apparatus could swivel in a 360°

arc, and the barrels could elevate themselves by forty degrees.

On paper, everything can exist.

Some animals had occasionally observed the emergence of various strange and rather mysterious objects from the ground between the concrete surface mound and the barbed wire parameter. One lizard in particular—a rather small fellow close to a foot and a half in length, perhaps ten pious pounds fat—once had been very disturbed about it. There he was, innocently soaking in the good June sun on a particularly fine day for lizards, on a particularly fine rock for lizards (he was rather racist), when all of a sudden (without warning mind you), the ground began tilting up!

At first he perceived it as a surrealistic mirage, the result of something he had eaten. But then the tilted earth sent him sprawling head over bent tail to the base of the rapidly forming perpendicular.

By the stance the lizard assumed after righting himself and finding himself in order, it appeared that he considered that sort of thing definitely uncalled-for!

A queer-shaped object rose slowly then above the banked perpendicular earth, and I'm very certain that the sign on it didn't satisfy the lizard, considering that the lizard didn't read, probably didn't want to read, and, in fact, never had any thoughts on the matter.

North Quadrant: C-42, Radio Antenna—Parabolic, the sign read.

The lizard decided that he'd take himself elsewhere and stalked off. Apparently, he did not like to be in places where sunning was not appreciated, where it was denied by tilting earths, crushed by unseen forces, and threatened by metal ghost giants of what the lizard may have considered to be his ancestors. The lizard had seen many skeletons in his limited time. It didn't seem to bother him that this one was made of aluminum, not an organic material—they were all the same in his eyes.

There are ruins in this desert other than those of the trees. I have seen them. Twenty-one miles south-southeast of the concrete surface mound, there are the outer fringes of what was once a vast major city of humanity.

The buzzards walk the streets now. Or fly through them.

From the air one can make out many steel reinforced walls that still stand within the city like statues, and they are thoroughly dead. Buzzards perch on them. They build their nests on the tops of them.

The world? It's very strange now, somewhat renaturalized now. Is it true that in some areas forests, although mutated, have taken over the cities? But not common? It is a long-time phenomenon, I admit.

A second a year and then a year a second.

. . . in the city here, the Republic, in the air pumped from the farms and pushed past the nose, one can feel the presence of unpleasant things . . .

In a totally dark, totally quiet, almost airtight sealed basement perhaps the mummy of somebody named . . . perhaps she sits in an old armchair with a basket of her laundry beside her once fresh from a dryer. She had made an attempt to dig her way out, had tired, sat down for a moment, and part of her had just walked away. Her eyes are closed as if in sleep or intimate prayer. She died of a lack of a certain air.

And her death mask is totally blank, devoid of any emotion. No bitterness, no resolution, no resignation; nothing.

. . . and the children . . .
. . . and the husband . . .
. . . and the new morality . . .
. . . and the life and resurrection . . .

farce
farce
farce

"Sir?"

Dust is probably settling in the cracks of somebody named . . . face . . .

"Sir?"

"Leave me alone," he said softly, yet distinctly from all reports.

"It is important, your majesty."

"Leave me alone!"

"But, my lord, perhaps you don't understand?"

"I need no understanding today!" he was heard to say. "I ask for none, and none will I give! Good day!"

"Sir . . ."

It was then that the servant's voice halted in mid-breath as his master rose up from his bed, got out, and stood beside it. What had upset the prince, no man was certain. His eyes were glistening, and that was an unusual event for the man, and yet they say there was a slight sort of smile on his lips. His cheeks were flushed. The servant told me later that the prince's hands were trembling—ill perhaps? They lacked a sense of coloration; the hands were shaking, pale.

Servant and prince stood silently in that finely furnished monster of a bedroom. They exchanged looks.

"Shall I seek a suitable punishment for this insubordination?" the prince said once, crisp and sharp.

Bowing, the servant left.

The bedroom became silent, quiet silence, with no indication of noise.

Yet there was always the whirl of the ventilation fans trapped somewhere in the background, but the mind quickly adapted to it as if it were a pulse or function of the natural body.

The carpet was lush shag, and the walls were paneled in hard walnut that had been carved by hand. The royal coat of arms hung on the wall that was facing the northeast. A tapestry depicting a forest hung on the opposite wall. The tapestry was a massive work—thirty-two by twenty feet. The bed was two hundred and thirty years old; some famous man was sure to have slept on it.

He knew all the parties that were in charge of spying. He had kept up his rewards. A few pieces of cash, a little honest graft permitted here and there . . .

There was a knock on the prince's door and a woman with a cross on her forehead, of about twenty-three years in age, her face in a perpetual professional heat, entered. "Would my master wish some entertainment?" she asked.

Very well-versed . . .

She told me that he told her to go to Hell.

She then left.

He was a good-looking prince, and his mother and father, whenever they thought of him, it is said, were quite proud of him. He was likened to be another John, first king of the Republic—the prince's great-great-grandfather. Indeed, from all the royal records both official and unofficial, of all the men that have succeeded to the throne the prince bore the closest resemblance to he who had started it all. He had the same brilliant blue eyes, the same hair and skin coloring —damp brown and clear Germanic white. If the prince differed, it was only in the lips and nose, and that was slight. He looked more serious than his ancestor. He was perhaps more self-centered.

He had a marvelously well-trained mind. He had received

the finest general education any man could want—he could understand most any discussion of any trade or art and possessed, some say, remarkable insight.

It was reported that after the woman left there came another knock at the prince's door. It was that eternally special knock, one that would look wrong in the public's eye for the prince to deny.

And the King's . . .

If not the Church . . .

And God . . .

He let the Archbishop of Wayne enter.

They say that Wayne always knocked in the same fashion, a fashion perhaps rather timid for such a large, rather overwhelming man. He stood about six feet in height, but weighed close to three hundred pounds. He was forty years of age. His hair had turned a solid gray, but all of it was there under the high hat of his office.

Baldness is the norm for men of his age, considering the common stock from whence Wayne had come.

"Wayne," the prince was heard to say.

"Peace be unto you, your majesty," Wayne answered.

At this point the prince cooled, obviously remembering his politics.

"I wasn't expecting you."

"You have problems, my son?"

Wayne told me that now, at this point, the prince cooled even further to him, was silent; then abruptly he turned toward his wine cabinet.

"Some wine, Archbishop?" the prince said after a long minute.

"One has habits, your majesty."

"Wine?"

"A little bit, thank you."

The prince served the Archbishop, motioning to one of the two armchairs that sat before his fake fireplace, and sat down in the other.

It is said that God drives the Archbishop. Or the Archbishop drives God. Wayne's mind was filled with religious platitudes, moralities, normalities. And the masses tended to look up to Wayne with passion in their hearts, their faces in a sort of heat, their voices panting out their prayers.

Some say that Wayne will make a fine Saint Peter for the new church and the new religion, though both subjects have a good hundred and eleven years of age to them.

No one in power can trust the Archbishop.

Perhaps they can see his ego drip off his blessed robes like

holy oil and pulsate through his body like pontifical sex—
lewd and forbidden. Under Wayne's Archbishop's staff, the
sheep of his Church have swollen in a unified body strong
enough to challenge even the state in the name of God.

. . . in the name of God . . .

. . . yet tradition . . .

. . . yet doubt . . .

. . . yet a sort of distorted faith . . .

The prince told the Archbishop that he was having strange
dreams.

The prince told me later that he saw Wayne fastening
upon his emotion like a sort of leech, and that the man, if
permitted, was perfectly willing to draw raw blood from it.

"Dreams, your majesty?"

"Are dreams a sin?" asked the prince in an odd sort of
recovery.

"That depends on the dream," said Wayne, "and the
dreamer."

The prince stared at Wayne for a second, then got up
from his chair and walked around a bit, in circles, parallel
strips—in a most total random. After a while, he stopped by
the mantel of the fireplace as if that were his first direction
and rested his left arm there.

"But not the dream itself?" demanded the prince as if no
time had passed at all. "Can a dream alone be a sin?"

"Can wine left in the bottle make a man drunk?"

"Are actions more honorable than intentions? Never mind
that, Wayne—I have this dream!"

"A nightmare, your majesty?"

Another silence.

"It's a very strange dream," the prince said finally. "A
series of dreams, really. They are so . . . so . . . they make
it so that I do not wish to sleep."

Now Wayne was quiet.

"I have the same problem," he said carefully after a moment. "Men in our positions, your majesty, always do."

The verbal temptation, the prince thought. The false self-
identification.

"They are not dreams of persecution, Father," he said.

"I was not speaking of that."

"Neither of murder. If it were simply death . . ." The
prince's voice lowered. "Well, death I can take; I can accept
death. Besides, Father, death doesn't exist, not in reality, for
it's just a mere transition."

"Have you prayed?"

"My mother," the prince whispered. "I have prayed to my mother."

"It is wrong to pray to the dead."

The prince looked away. "But she hasn't died," he said.

"Has the physician. . . ?"

"To *Hell* with the physician!"

A shiver seemed to pass through the prince's body as if ice had been poured through the bundled fibers of his spinal cord. He closed his eyes for a moment. His face became very pale.

"Forgive me, Father," the prince said calmly enough after a period of two minutes had elapsed. He opened his eyes, breathing deeply. "I have sinned," he said.

"We are all sinners, my son."

"Yes." The prince laughed nervously. "We are, aren't we?"

"Our goal in life is to overcome that."

"Why did you come here, Wayne?"

"To see your majesty."

"Uninvited?"

"We have our duties, my lord."

"For what purpose, then?"

"For your purpose, your majesty. To be available to you if you have need of me."

Wayne said that this seemed to satisfy the prince for a moment, and that the man kept standing by the fireplace with his left arm on the mantel, sipping the wine from the goblet he held in his right hand, the synthetic version shining artificially red in the cut crystal glass. . . .

The silence came complete. The light was solid, the flow of the artificially filtered air solid, the shine of the immaculately clean room solid. . . .

"How like God you are," said the prince.

"What?"

"Oh." The prince laughed. "Do you need explanation? We are all made in His image, are we not? In His mud and from it, are we not? Though we differ between ourselves, it is said, by the color of the skin and the shape of the nose and the hair, we are all in His likeness, are we not? In my mind, you, I . . . I swear, the entire human race—we are all copies of the most divine Father! Therefore, my dear Archbishop, how like God you are."

"You seem feverish," Wayne said. "Have you seen the royal physician?"

"Yes. I have. The buffoon. The doctor . . . what's-his-name . . . yes."

"What did Dr. Barton say?"

"That I should rest. And eat more; I'm losing weight. He said that nothing's the matter—nothing's wrong with me . . . that I have no appetite because I upset my stomach with my brain. That I should rest . . . what did you expect? I *have this illusion!*"

Wine falling, the prince fell on his knees before the Archbishop as the drops fell over him—he buried his face within the depths of his hands; his body shook.

The Archbishop said that he then asked the prince whether or not he desired to confess.

"If only you can understand," the prince cried. "I dream that I'm lying in bed. A man that I know not appears at my bedroom door—one of the guards? I don't see his rank. He takes me up to one of the observation posts. Outside, Wayne, outside people are there! Naked people! Five miserable men! And they're pounding on the observation dome! They're screaming!"

"Is that all?"

The prince uncovered his face. He was silent for a long moment again. He stared out beyond the Archbishop to nowhere—an unfocused stare.

"We are all sinners, Father," he said finally.

"Is that all?" Wayne repeated.

"No," the prince told him quite calmly. "I was able to read the lips of a man on the outside. He was staring in as he pounded in a most odd way, Father, and screaming his vile temper at me."

"What did he say?"

The prince rose to his feet, laughing in an odd fashion. During the confession, the Archbishop had placed one of his hands on the prince's head. It was clammy and wet with sweat; drunk in it.

"Father," the prince said to the Archbishop. "He was calling me a bastard."

# II

A tangle of carrots fell from a storage bin—the bottom of a continual load from the Level 10 and 11 farms, little bits of dust still clinging to their white, tiny roots. In the factory's lights, machinery whirling, the carrots gleamed their respective brilliant orange colors; the thick artificial mud that had given them birth with water had been washed away—else they were hydroponic carrots, and lacked that flavor. . . .

". . . There's nothing to do but sit and watch," sang an idiot down the production line of machines.

Somewhere else, chunks of compressed reprocessed steel were brought forth from the Big Fall, bits and pieces slamming together; they all fell together into furnaces. In a white-hot stream the product emerged, ready to be cast, or hardened, or rolled—vaporous in its man-made lust; cooling, cooling in the cold air.

The carrots fell into a hot scalding bath whose clear, steamy depths were purified once every five minutes—the carrots stayed there for one minute before the wire bucket rose to toss them out. From there, the carrots fell down into another stainless steel chute to another platform of production.

In well-oiled, halting circles, the unborn circuitry boards spun about under the "chip" machines, stopping for perhaps a large fraction of a second before the maws of the machines to have a bit of micro-micro-printed circuitry, all siliconed and coppery, implanted in their willing frames.

. . . the validity of his birth has been established . . .

"The machines do it all, bastards; sit and watch."

The almost perpetual stream of carrots, miniature logs, all sizes and shapes, clean and glistening, were shuffled by the proper devices here and there, and finally through a grinding, noisy machine. They emerged from it on a sanitary rub-

17

beroid belt neatly sliced, diced, or grated—whatever the purpose.

". . . then why didn't the Queen produce another? God knows she had the time . . ."

"You can't have no woman without no pay . . ."

The rubberoid belts—they were black in color and driven by a nuclear fusion produced electricity—sped the carrots into high steam pressure cookers. Loads from tons to mere pounds were ready to be eaten in a moment's time—fully-prepared. From the steam pressure cookers, they were sent piping hot down other proper stainless steel chutes, sorted by their cut and quantity.

"No dollars will buy me no wine today."

A stream of plastic cans ran beside the idiot who sat and sang on a stool to himself. Occasionally, a supervisor walked by. Occasionally, a crushed, tattered plastic can came on its way to the final topping and irradiation devices. Occasionally, there came a can not full of product or with obvious impurities messing around in it. These the idiot picked up and deposited in a bin beside himself that stank of rotting carrot.

"Watch it, boys; see that it stays in the line."

The good cans moved to places mysterious to the idiot, through archways over which panels glowed with green lights that never changed. The line never halted. The carrots may have changed to beets or beans or cabbage or corn or the like, but the line never stopped. Sometimes they ran two products together, like sliced turnips in one can and green peppers in the other can—the turnips the even, the peppers the odd—but those were the rare times when the idiot had two bins to fill.

"Sit down on your ass," the idiot sang to no one, maybe wiping his nose every once in a while, "and do your time."

The carrots are canned.
The carrots are canned.

"Tell me, James," the prince said, walking along with me beside the silent growing rows of vegetation in the East Quadrant 11 farms area, the bright artificial sunlight hiding one of the secondary blast ceilings that topped every one of the fifteen levels. "Tell me," he repeated. "Did you ever find out where God lives?"

"My lord?" I said.

"What, no tongue? Hiding something, eh? Don't want us mortals to know?"

"Surely you're not serious, my lord?"

"Not really," he replied. "Mmm, the air's too fresh here."

"A marvelous freshness," I said.

A tender robot whirled by us, all gray metal and steel. It was spraying a mist on one of the rows to the right of us—it was a row of tomato plants just recently planted. Their likeness to their adult kin was evident in the greenness of the leaves in the man-made solar conditions; they grow very large and very swiftly, they say.

"What is space really, James?" the prince said after a while.

"A vacuum, your highness," I told him.

"This suspended animation you endured—was it painful?"

"To awaken is always painful, my lord; the body loves its rest. It's not so much painful, suspended animation, than it is very dangerous. I was told that I had a fifty percent chance of injury by it."

"And death?"

"Ten percent, although all these figures depended on the individual constitution."

"You like to take chances, don't you?"

"The entire universe," I replied, "is a vacuum, my lord. We are merely imperfections within it."

"You have a remarkable way of flattering the ego."

"I speak only to serve my lord."

"And serve only to speak?"

"That reaction is highly endothermic."

"You speak always with cause?"

"Always, my lord. And by your leave, of course."

"Yes, James," the prince said, laughing softly, "by my leave."

We moved on from a section of rows of vegetables whose lengths stretched almost to the limits of human vision into a section of grass. Most of the meat consumed in the Republic was in actuality a spun soybean product, with the exception of the royal herd kept in a section of the North Quadrant farms. This grass was a very special kind of grass. It was planted through the few recreation areas in the city, and in the city arena which was rarely used. This grass produced an abnormal amount of oxygen per blade, for it was a controlled mutation. It was a hardy type of grass; people were permitted to walk on it, although few held that desire. Fourteen thousand of humanity walked the streets of the Republic, which was filled to less than half its capacity—the seven parks were almost always deserted. Some organized sports were conducted there, but then those were for the young. There were bars for the male thirty-nine percent of the population, and of course there were the ever-popular brothels where the surplus women—inspected, blessed, and certified by the Church—took profit from their bodies. These were adult games; the Church and its establishment made their money from their strictly licensed operation. These were adult delights.

I sat down with the prince.

We stretched out on the deliberately long, fresh-smelling luxury, and if we desired a tan all we had to do was strip, for the lights here were proper enough; but tans in the Republic were uncommon burns.

"What are you to tell me?" the prince droned, sticking a long blade of grass in his mouth.

"Considering that I'm your advisor on military affairs, my lord," I said, "and I might add, your *new* military advisor, it is more my duty that I answer your questions than to lecture. Your father, need I remind you, has placed me by your side for that purpose, and to assist you in times of emergency."

"Ah, yes," the prince mocked. "Yes."

"Well, I myself would rather stand a full tour of watches, my . . ."

"What's it like up there?" the prince shot back.

I stopped my thought for a moment's passage.

"There?" I said. "Where?"

"Not space," answered the prince immediately. "I've had enough of that for a while; no, I'm asking about ground surface. They told me they picked up your body a few miles west-northwest from here—you must have had a glance at something those few miles."

"A ruin," I said.

"Really?"

"Oh, not all. I landed in a stand of trees, some oak, hemlock, pine. Maybe some maple—I'm no expert on trees. I landed within a small opening in that forest, but, my lord, once I had gone one mile closer to the Republic, well, the land surrounding the Republic is horribly bleak."

"So they say."

"I orbited the Earth for eleven days before I decided to come down. The *Stellar's* still up there, sir; I took the landing craft, and that's damaged beyond repair now. The landing was a bit hard."

"I see," the prince said.

"No, I do not think you can, my lord," I said. "I was supposed to land in the Pacific if, for some reason, the space stations were not up. They weren't, of course. I was supposed to contact the Space Exploration Lab in Sands, New Mexico, for instructions. No answer. I orbited the Earth for eleven days, my lord, and I didn't see any sign of surface habitation anywhere."

"Oh," the prince said softly.

"The opening in the forest? It used to be a parking lot, my lord. There were walls hidden in the trees; I had landed in a suburb of what used to be Detroit—the body of the city they say is in the desert. Eleven days . . . I'd rather not say more."

"Nor do the guards," the prince said. "They won't let me out in a radiation suit for a personal investigation; they're afraid of even the slightest damage to the *royal genes.*"

"I see," I said.

"No," the prince said. "You don't. But that doesn't matter, James. What star did you visit, now?"

"Bernard's Star."

"Did you find anything of interest?"

"Some planets, of course. The five were uninhabitable."

"Oh."

"I gave the results of my exploration to the King's men. They seemed delighted with it."

"They all seem that way with all matters, all matters to them being quite worthless, trivial things."

"Yes, they do, don't they?"

We were quiet for another moment, and I followed the prince in picking up a piece of grass. It tasted earthy and refreshing.

"In private," the prince said, "drop the polite phrases. My Christian name is Robert."

"All right, Robert."

"That's better. . . . They have you standing watches already? How long have you been here?"

"Six weeks."

"Six weeks and I didn't hear about it until only two weeks ago? Where have they been hiding you?"

"In the Military College."

"Really, now?"

"Two weeks ago, Robert, the King gave me my knighthood and my *wealth;* I didn't ask for a penny but he granted it to me anyway. I was under the care and training of senior General William H. Handerlaan—our most loyal, though senile, defender. Let me not be trite: They had me swearing an oath of allegiance to the Republic as soon as they had my spacesuit off, they had me converted to the Church as I showered—Wayne the Archbishop did so himself—and they were teaching me the defenses of the Republic as soon as I was verified by what documents I had brought with me, and the little smattering of history that has remained with us."

"Who's to say you're not a spy?" said the prince.

"Yes, who's to say?"

The prince chuckled at what appeared to be his own personal joke and, as he did so, looked about at the scenery. Mounted on the ceiling some thirty-five feet up, a series of various robotic devices planted seeds in the plots that had recently been harvested, sprayed various high intensity fertilizers into others, and laid in still other, more barren areas a black stream of artificially prepared dirt—a muck more productive than common ground. Floor robots ran about with red lights on the tops of their heads cultivating the soil, their treads making odd marks on the ground. And occasionally one would see a man. But there was no man close to us. Perhaps the nearest man was about five hundred yards away, in the exact center of the level—in a circular office there. When we had passed him on the way to the tomatoes, we had observed him with his feet up on a control desk having a cup of coffee as the computers buzzed away.

"Do you like it here?" the prince said suddenly.

"What, my lord?"

"The name's Robert. Do you like it here in the Republic?"

"What do you mean, Robert?"

"*Here,* James. I mean, it's only a city, but . . . this life. Isn't it any different from the one you left?"

"I like it here, your majesty," I said carefully.

"In what fashion?"

"In that it's still the same as the world I left except for the names, Robert."

"A difficult switch of loyalties, is that it?"

"No."

The prince shook his head. "Tell me later then," he said.

The prince stretched completely out on the grass now, closing his eyes. For about five minutes he said nothing. I touched the grass. The musk of its product filled my sense of smell. The grass touched back.

"James," the prince said from the ground when the time had passed. "Tell me about the defensive setup of the Republic." Then he sat up and stared at me.

"Checking my homework?"

"You guessed correctly, James."

"There are four basic defense systems," I began, "routed through Defense Command. That's the joint with the lousy coffee I have to spend eight hours a week in. It's located on Level fifteen, you know, that expansion level under the factories. The systems, get these original names, are called the long or number one, middle or number two, short or number three, and absolute or number four defensive systems.

"The long system is a parameter of weaponry that is placed at the outer limits of the Republic just above Level one. It's about a thousand yards out from the surface installation or surface mound as some call it. The long system consists of, besides various small arms emplacements which are never used unless an invasion threatens—it consists of twenty standard M/C cannon. There are five cannon per quadrant, each with an atmospheric range of twenty miles. They all have variable power settings, controlled either by substation emplacements or Defense Command, ranging from a blanket pulsation stun for ground troops to full power which can tear a ten-foot wide hole through five-inch thick steel plate. That is, of course, if the plate's unshielded.

"Thank God that magnetic shielding equipment is heavy enough to require a massive plane to carry it, or a heavy tank; I'd hate to think what we'd do if someone developed a way to cut that ten-ton weight requirement.

"Oh," I stopped. "I take it you realize that an M/C cannon is not really a refinement of a sealed transmission laser, but is a form of matter conversion weaponry, being essentially a projector of magnetically shielded anti-energy quanta."

The prince nodded.

"The long system's weaponry is stored—well, in fact, everything's retracted to below-surface compartments able to take a near direct one-megaton blast. They are raised to the surface for use. The cannon can swivel in a full, three hundred and sixty degree arc with a ninety degree elevation. Of course, they can't be fired into the surface installations without first being removed from the Defense Computer System, and that requires extensive rewiring."

"Go on," the prince said.

"The middle system is located about five feet in front of the outermost pavement circle on the surface—the access road that runs around the surface mound that was originally intended for surface supply. We now use it as a staging ground whenever we send out a *LandHov* surface party.

"The middle system contains the same amount of weaponry as the long, though of course more concentrated. Ten of its cannon are M/C fifty-ones, a dual standard weapon with about twice the power of the normal M/C thirties, our standards.

"The middle system can be lowered even farther than the long—to below the Republic's primary blast roof, giving them a ten-megaton direct blast handling capability.

"The short system is a last-ditch defense system composed of surface light weapons mounted in the surface mound. We store our anti-tank, anti-personnel, and SRBM nuclear warhead missiles there, along with four batteries of ten dual-barreled, thirty-millimeter automatic cannon. The short system, of course, can stand a full ten-megaton surface blast without significant damage."

"And the fourth defensive system?" questioned the prince.

"The absolute," I said, "is contained in the Republic's only external defense center, five miles north. It's connected with the city by subway. It houses our ABM equipment, both missiles and launchers, and a limited amount of offensive weaponry."

"Limited?"

"Twenty ICBM with twenty-megaton warheads; fifteen IRBM with twenty-megaton warheads."

"Hydrogen fusion?"

"Hydrogen fusion, except that they all can be jacketed," I said.

"And all of this is controlled by the Defense Computer System? And Defense Command?"

"Well," I went on, "in a sense nothing is. Defense Command is essentially a supervisor—all parts of each system have their own private crews—and there are five substations for independent control if Defense Command is knocked out. But normally, out of convenience, Defense Command controls all."

I had finished.

The prince, seeing this, turned over on his stomach, rubbed his nose in the grass, then looked up at me.

"You know what?" he said.

"What?"

"I believe I can trust you, James."

"My father told me never to trust anyone no matter how sincere, Robert."

"Not even a prince?"

"Not even a king."

And so the trust became a brief complete silence.

And the air, the very air, seemed perhaps purified by it.

"So space is a vacuum," the prince muttered.

And I said nothing.

"And Jesus was a bastard, then."

What an odd . . .

"A bastard?"

"Oh," the prince replied, laughing so much that his stomach shook. "I didn't mean to blaspheme, James, but the seed that sprung Him was not Joseph's seed."

"Of course not! It was God's."

"Therefore: His son had to be a bastard."

"Impossible!"

But then I thought a moment more. "Oh," I said. "I see your direction, and yet we are all married to the Church and to God."

"So I believe," replied the prince, "but tell me then, for argument's sake, does it mean that when a man marries a woman, that the man and woman in question are committing a double bigamy?"

"You must be insane, Robert."

"No, not really," the prince laughed back, "but by our dictionary, Mary was an adulteress or at least a bigamist and therefore her Son—a bastard. 'Tis no dishonor by it."

"But the Birth was a special case!"

"Well done, James!" the prince cried. "We can throw our dictionaries out on that one, can't we?"

"What do you mean?"

"I don't want to discuss," the prince said slowly, deliberately, "His reasons as to why He had Jesus come to the planet through the womb of a most Holy Virgin. I merely want to discuss the gross stupidity displayed at times through the actions of the self-named 'thinking man.' "

"The intellectual?"

A very low-pitched blower went on. It breathed stale air from the public corridors through the hungry grass. The prince and I got up and headed south through a row of carrots.

"Not the true intellectuals," the prince continued. "They are rather mystical, for they will not admit their genius. They hide themselves very well. I mean the ones that stand on impure, perhaps ridiculous, qualifications that our fathers and ourselves have set up from prejudice."

"Go on."

The prince reached down, pulled a carrot from the ground,

the mud giving it up; it was ripe or very close to it. He brushed the dirt off the vegetable, and together we headed toward one of the few human water fountains placed in the farms levels to wash it off. I followed.

"Let this carrot, for example, represent a man," he said. "And don't laugh, James; some men are vegetables in more than physical matters. The carrot is, by the way, a most thoughtful plant—it displays a sort of weedy, unappetizing top to the sun, leaving its most sweet, luscious parts underground where they—or it, being three parts as a whole—can not be seen. Like the true intellectual, the carrot doesn't mind mud or water or earthy things—it loves them for they are its elements; both the carrots and the intellectuals. Neither do they neglect their birthplace or themselves; backgrounds, families, small matters mean nothing to them both. Look here, James; isn't this carrot beautiful?"

It was spattered with the black, artificial dirt. Parts of its kinetic orange skin shone through.

"It's natural," I said.

"The most beautiful aspects of life are the most natural. We can only enhance that beauty or destroy it."

"Yes," I said.

We reached the water fountain and I held my hand over the photo-switch so that the water would pour while the prince cleaned his carrot.

"There," he said once he was done. "It's perhaps more beautiful now, is it not? Enhanced? All clean and ready for consumption?"

"Yes."

"Is it perhaps more beautiful than when it had mud over it?"

"Of course."

"Oh!" the prince mocked. "That certain expression on your lips; that air of absolute decision on your breath! How can you be so positive? It's the same carrot, is it not? How can it be more beautiful? Beautiful is not really a comparative adjective."

"Your philosophy would seem to indicate that marble left in the ground is in a better state than an artist's finished product."

"In this case, conception has occurred."

"Well, in any event, you've washed the mud off."

"I've washed the mud off of it! Such observation! Such intellectual ability, James!"

"Well, by washing the mud off a man you can certainly make some improvement," I said.

"Is that man really improved?" countered the prince. "How can we, or society to be honest, determine whether or not he's dirty? It all depends on the observer, and the man in question."

"The proper woman's better than the common whore," I said.

"Is she really?" replied the prince. "The whore has reasons for her actions; the proper woman may never."

"I still say . . ."

"That the proper woman's better? Do a piece of paper and an undying devotion—phenomena that admittedly are quite rare these days—do they justify an act of sex better than money?"

"Certainly."

"So much so that a married woman caught in poor circumstance should never go to bed with another man—'tis un-Godly and impure—even in order to save the life of her husband from the hands of vile and dastardly kidnappers. A breach of faith is more prohibitive than that of life."

"I didn't say that!"

"Oh, in a way you did, James. For given that circumstance that wife is a whore, if we are to hold to our definitions, and the saved husband should reluctantly sue for adultery."

The prince smiled and bounced the carrot in his hand.

"Don't believe in words here, James. They may have meant something quite valuable in the past, but not in the Republic; the air is filled with cheats. Don't believe in words —they are an illusion. Accept only those that are proven; in others wait patiently but wisely for their testing. Don't believe in paper here, either. Whereas a blank sheet is real, the ink upon it is not. Men use their power as erasers quite well here. Believe in friendship, in men and their observable actions. I don't mean ignoring the prattling of fools—fools can be the wisest of men at times—but place all in its proper perspective. Believe in men, for words, both written and verbal, can be twisted to make the most high and holy object appear to be the most low and damnable. They can also do the reverse, and make the most horrid bastard—king.

"Men are not observers, James," he said. "Men are the observed."

# III

They line up the guilty against the perpetually clean walls of the Church of the Just, the monks of the Holy Guard of the Cross do. All kneel as the opening prayers are chanted before a full-color statue of Jesus caught at His death on the Cross; the Man pinned to the staining wood, the blood full evident and caught in mid-drip; the need for justice a darkening in His crystal eyes.

". . . In the name of our Lord, Amen," chants the presiding priest, his amplified voice ringing throughout the vast polished hall, reverberating against the stained glass from whence artificial sunlight seems to shine. And as the sound travels, a small robed boy holds the prayer book aloft, arms quivering under the massive weight of it; all of this is really unnecessary for the priest—he memorized the proper procedures long ago.

Swords displayed and gleaming, they, the monks, line up the guilty against the cream-colored polished walls, the wooden panels depicting the journey of Jesus to the place of the Skulls above their heads, the what-appears-to-be stone floor under their feet. They try each case individually, the priests do, before our God and their pocketbook and the political consequences; then determine the proper punishment.

The royalty's above the proper crime.

The monks, enrobed—they line up the guilty against the walls, the daily one hundred or so. The murderers, the thieves, the adulteresses and male counterparts, the divorce cases, the civil suits, the heretics, the blasphemers; the breakers of the Church's law; the guilty who deny the truth.

The priests sanction Life.

Death.

Afterdeath.

They redeem.

They kill.

They excommunicate.

They judge the right from the wrong when cases call for such a judgment.

Occasionally, they grant a divorce.

". . . In the name of our Lord, Amen," chants the presiding priest.

They accept all confessions, and will chant the proper prayers as the murderers are led off to be hanged or gassed or poisoned. The redeemed are given a choice before the Big Fall.

Adultery—never.

The primary penalty for sex with an unblessed woman—that is, a woman who is not married to the man, or a Church-licensed prostitute—is a public flogging to both parties of ten lashes, each, in the city arena.

The second—twenty.

The third—excommunication and death by beheading; a monk's sword is employed.

The priests are wealthy men.

And so are the monks in their lesser ways.

The guilty are the gullible.

The guilty are, sometimes, men with undesirable idealism who are poor or unsponsored, and have attacked the Church.

The Court is for show.

The monks of the Holy Guard administer the necessary police duties, and maintain order in the Republic and Church by the use of their ceremonial swords, which are carefully anointed each morning with the blessed oil, and prayed over by the abbot of their order. They wear personnel mines under their robes, and occasionally body armor. Each monk has a tiny, tiny radio implanted in his chest cavity which is operated by mysterious flexes of his right arm. Each monk has a laser pistol strapped under his left armpit. His sword is sharp, and each monk knows its employment.

The minor criminals repent, are forgiven, spend a day or week in the jail in service to the Lord, go out, and eventually sin again. They return, are blessed, spend another day or week . . .

Those who commit crimes of undue violence usually find themselves one morning quite dead.

". . . In the name of our Lord, Amen," chants the presiding priest.

The sweat, silver in the Church's light, trembles for a moment, then slides off the small boy's forehead, dripping on the artificial stone floor.

They line up the guilty for trial.

They line up the guilty . . .
They . . .
They


The garbage of the masses is flung down individual stainless steel chutes, washed away with greenish, oily liquid to
the larger tunnels of the unseen bottoms of each level, and
then to the Big Fall.

A large shaft, fifty yards in diameter, pierces through each
level of the Republic. It houses some of the power lines,
communication lines, ventilation shafts, two massive freight
elevators, and the Big Fall.

The large shaft of the Big Fall is shielded and braced to
withstand a direct, twenty-megaton surface blast. It is exactly twenty-one yards in diameter.

The wastes tumble into the Big Fall, and then to the "fires"
below. In an almost perpetual rain, almost all the matter
ever realized in the Republic, the remains of every product
created in the Republic, fall to their purging in green liquid-
coated masses.

But it is not a true fall.

It is a precisely regulated fall.

It is a fall controlled by artificial gravity fields.

It is a gravitation fall, precise, to fill demands.

The "flame" at the bottom licks up and consumes it all.

The fire, housed in a magnetic field and shielded by lead,
is never seen by human eyes except those of the dead falling down the Big Fall, coated in the green liquid, to their
most total dismemberment.

In the "flame" every atom tears apart from every other—
every molecular bond is broken.

Then the light and heavy and middle and all in-between
elements are separated. . . .

And new raw materials are formed. . . .

They stimulate the fire with plutonium, uranium, and
other such remarkable metals. They build up the necessary
heat and add hydrogen which they extract in the necessary
amounts from water occasionally piped in forty miles from
Lake Saint Clare.

In other words, they foster the birth and continue the life
of a tiny sun where all is purified.

And then they dip magnetic cups into the broth of that sun
and the proper devices drink from it.

The men watch electronic afterimages on their monitor
screens as the machinery, in a sort of technical union, react.

The lead is very thick, and the magnetic shielding very strong.

And thermocouples produce a tremendous part of the Republic's commercial electrical power, while breeder reactors elsewhere produce the surplus and the rest.

Electricity.

Power.

Power.

. . . in reality, the prince said, bending over his artificial fireplace, the electrical glow washing over his deep-shadow-darkened face. In reality, I have no position of command unless my father . . .

"You say my son has got worse in his affliction?" the King was reported to cry, sitting on a small throne in his private chamber, his hair very gray and his face wrinkled in disgust of time.

"Unfortunate, my lord," said Wayne, "but I fear it is a strong possibility."

"Wayne," demanded the King, "how can this be? My only son, never strong with me, but my only son—apart."

. . . his body at sixty in fine physical condition, his heart's very strong; they say he's good for another thirty . . .

"He seems to be suffering under some sort of illness," said Wayne. "His behavior is perhaps . . . irrational?"

"Has he confessed?" asked the King.

"He has, my lord," replied a monk, a Brother Conrad Gates.

"What does he speak of?"

"That, my lord, is between myself and God, but I can tell you this: He indeed is a man who is struggling with his soul."

"To the point of damnation?"

Gates gave a slight smile. "No," he said. "He is merely insecure."

"We must hear reports from those who surround him," said the King. "Has the physician been called?"

"Not by the prince, your majesty," said Gates.

"By me, my lord," Wayne replied. "He believes, as do I, that it may be an illness of the mind. . . ."

"My son is mad?"

". . . And I detest my father," the prince said, taking the wine I held out for him.

"Why?" I asked casually.

"Let me set you straight, James. This entire life—I smell something strange here that I do not like. My mother dead before I'm five years of age. I hate my father, for he never sees me; nay, I am forbidden the celebration of the Mass in his presence."

"What?"

"Don't you understand? I've been under the hands of my tutors and peers all my life; I am permitted the company of the King only during certain ceremonial functions."

"Such as?"

"His birthday, James; my birthday: Christmas, Easter, and Republic days of royal honor—when he sees fit to declare them."

"That's . . ."

"It averages out to twelve times a year, James—about an hour each time. We are human men. We sit, garbed in all our splendor, which makes me sweat like a bitch, while the stereovision cameras scan our beauty and we make polite off-camera conversation for show as the orchestra drags on and the parade goes by and through the arena."

"I see."

"No, James," the prince said forcefully, placing his empty wine glass down firmly on the opulent false mantel of his fake fireplace. "You can not."


. . . but if I remarry?

. . . God says that each ruler must be male as was His Son Jesus, therefore even if your majesty were to remarry, she would not be able to assume the throne if your son, let us say, proves defective?

. . . defective . . .

. . . yes, my lord, but fit to carry down the line . . .

. . . madness does not breed?

. . . this madness does not breed, my lord . . .


The names on the doors look like those of lawyers. Only the age barrier, really not observed, distinguishes them from the rest.

A worker from the factory, filthy from his labor, pauses before a door, a well-lighted door, and counts his donation before he enters.

The light goes out.

He will emerge, purified, one hour later.

Some walk the streets dressed as any woman would, the scent of their profession awash in the ventilated air.

"Your place or mine?"

"No, forgive me, not today."

"Fully blessed . . ."

"I can see that. Good day, my lady."

The ravished cross across hot foreheads smeared . . .

Running, the children attack the playrooms, devastating the swings. One looks up at the blue painted ceiling while most fight mock battles on the ground.

"Orphans."

"Born of the women?"

"Born of those women."

"Why . . ."

"Contraception? With our underpopulation and terrible birthrate?"

"What . . ."

"They marry, James? They never own what they produce out of wedlock—they're fertile; they'll make their own."

"But . . ."

"Few seem to marry anyway."


. . . yet I say, reads the priest over the silent congregation, that if I, or an angel of Heaven were to preach to you any other gospel than the one you have heard, may he be damned! You have heard me say it before, and now I put it down in black and white—may anyone who preaches any other gospel than the one you have already be a damned soul!

Amen

Amen


"Robert?"

"James," he said finally, "why must I be such a bastard?"

"We all are."

"We are?"

"If we are images of God, then it must be so by our dictionary."

He smiled briefly, then stared down into the fake electrical fire that slowly stepped upon the synthetic logs within.

"Father," he muttered.

"What?"

He laughed. "It's funny," he said, "but at this moment, I wish that my father . . ."

"Don't we all, my lord," I said from the armchair. "Mine's a hundred and thirty years gone."

"And mine," sighed the prince, very quietly, very calmly, "is an eternity of times away."

# IV

---

"... oh, but he's in a bad mood, sir," the guard said.

I had found him, a face that I had seen somewhere else at some other time in the past, guarding a single door that led off a small corridor. It was the small corridor, number eight, that ran into the north-to-south main transport tunnel of the first level. The surface, and this was the closest point one could unofficially come to it, was one hundred and twenty feet above our heads. Twenty-four feet from our heads was a false ceiling that hid the inner layer of the massive main blast roof from view, besides auxiliary ventilation pipes, water and power pipes, and other such delights. The walls separating the compartments of this level of the city, the small stores, offices, auxiliary warehouses, military installations, were very, very thick for massive blast-absorbing coils were buried within them.

Entrance to North Quadrant Surface Observation, the sign on the door read; the door was a massive metal slab. Authorized Personnel Only.

"... but he's in a bad mood, sir," the guard said.

The guard wore the unremarkable blue uniform of his division: the Second Division Armor-Infantry. It consisted of a one-piece bodystocking-type suit that ran from toe to turtleneck. Around his waist he wore a wide black belt with a most ceremonial laser pistol strapped to his right hip. He cradled a full M/C-34 mass rifle which he held outward with his left arm against his belt; apparently he was issued that higher powered weapon (the M/C-32 being the standard), for he was guarding what was considered a high security area.

Being not so dedicated or permanent, the soldiers did not rate implanted radios; a wrist radio was all too evident on this guard's left wrist. The antenna wire gleamed silvery on his left wrist sleeve—it was impregnated in the cloth of his uniform. His helmet was as blue as his uniform, the color of blue the sky once held, with a black visor that the guard kept very clean. Day and night. He was a corporal in rank, this being indicated by the two black slashes on his sleeves. His boots, reaching toward his knees, were very black, perhaps even blacker than his helmet visor, and made of a leather-like synthetic. It was much more elastic than the artificially-made real thing; it tightly gripped the foot and ankle, but gave a runner much more mobility.

". . . he's in a bad mood, sir," the guard said.

My next visit with the prince will be at nine o'clock tomorrow morning, I thought. I have a watch from 0500 to 0900 in the Defense Command. . . .

Tonight, I needed sleep. I had tried to obtain it; failing, I went for a calming walk. . . .

. . . The *news* had informed the public that there had been a shutdown of one of the air purification blowers for its regular overhaul in Level 1. Air quality, they said, had dropped by five percent. But it was still basically fresh.

. . . As an officer, my uniform? I am permitted a coat, oh most holy of holies! The guard can see my rank, it's plain on my shoulders, and he can see the gold and purple sash of my knighthood. It runs from my right shoulder exactly to the left side of my waist. And the Republic's seal, the crown above the upright scroll of the gospels, surrounded by the two standing griffins, and the motto: *de profundis*. The guard can see my so-called authority . . . my grand illusion.

. . . The air, a difference? They say that five percent is never enough, but isn't there a stuffiness that even in these high corridors, that even the more massive halls, of this level of the Republic can not crush?

". . . in a bad mood," the guard said.

This city is only half filled, and yet the city planners on the first and second levels are expanding those levels outward all the time. Perhaps this is their way of insuring full employment among the thirty-nine percent male population which controls all. And whoredom for the enslaved women, or clerks' roles until physical equality is reached?

There is a shift rush every four hours, but now, in this night, it is a most total quiet. . . .

A streetwalker passed after the guard had uttered his phrase; she was perhaps a novice to the trade, for she appeared no more than sixteen or seventeen years old. She advertised her wares as we both watched, her pleasant hips undulating before us most professionally, and the subtle trace of a smile. They are curious women, these who grow to hate men. The sign crafted into her dress read "Follow me," and her feet were clean. To purchase one . . . not now, not tonight. The blessing of the Church, that cross on her forehead, she's legal at least; that did not make it right. Working her way through a college. Perhaps Scripture's scrawled across her belly so her lover in cash can expand his mind while emptying his lust?

"My," the guard sighed.

"The King's in a bad mood, you say?" I said after the whore had disappeared around a corner.

The guard, nodding in an abstract way, smiled a bit, then took out a cigarette, thereby breaking the no smoking rule while on duty. I held my lighter out for him, he lit the cigarette, and exhaled a thanks; the gray smoke lifted up in the air.

"I have a friend who's on the King's guard," he said. Then he waved his illegality around to make certain the validity of his assumption.

"Of course," I said, "no mention. What of that friend now? What does he do?"

"Oh, various things," the guard said, relaxing fully now. "Guard duty, of course—occasionally some errands; pretty soft. You know . . . now hey, that's got me a'thinking—there's this maid on the King's staff, sir. Well, sir, she's got the most marvelous set of buttocks that man has ever delighted within."

"This would place the King in a bad mood?"

"That? Oh no, sir! I wasn't talking about that in reference to the King, sir!"

"You're a draftee soldier?"

"Yes, sir."

"Figures."

"Yes, sir," he said, taking another puff of his cigarette. "But that maid, sir . . ."

"I agree: the maid's a much better topic."

"So do the rest of the King's guards, sir, so my friends tell me, sir."

Another cloud of gray fragrant smoke.

"You have more than one friend in association with the King?"

"That maid, sir, for one," he said.

"Oh, now." I laughed. "Something's going up, here?"

"Or down, or by the side, or upside down," said the guard.

"You should be ashamed of yourself."

"But she's so easily obtainable, sir!"

"You don't say?"

"Of course, sir." The guard added as an aside: "Unblessed, but considering the temptation, sir . . ."

"Watch your zipper, soldier," I said. "I give you friendly warning."

"Oh." The guard laughed. "Don't worry, sir. We have a pool."

"A pool?"

"Yes, of, let us say, bail money?"

"Bail money."

"The average price is about two hundred, sir, depending of course on the priest."

"I see. What about the girl?"

"We pay to keep her out too, sir. Besides, not many know."

"Except God."

"Sir?"

"Never mind."

"Oh."

Another puff.

"What's this about the King, now?" I said finally.

"Him? Oh, he's too old for that sort of shoddy thing, don't you think, sir?

"Say," he continued, his eyes brightening. "Would you like the maid's number?"

"Thank you," I said, laughing, "but no. I have my own sources. However, if they should dry up?"

We both laughed.

"Seriously now," I said, taking a puff of the cigarette which he now offered me. "What's this about the King?"

"Oh, he's been firing cooks, sir."

"Oh, really?"

" 'Find me a decent cook!' he screams," the guard said. "But they ain't found one yet to please him."

"Hmm."

"He keeps them for about a month, you see, and then he fires them. They say he's grown awfully sensitive lately as to the way he takes his meals. Can't seem to take meat too well, and vegetables—forget it. They have to feed him real red meat all the time instead of the normal stuff, even though no one can taste the difference. The King can taste the difference. It's been hell on the royal herd, sir; they been using fertility drugs and they can't keep up. I daresay, sir, no cook in the Goddamn world has the talents to keep the King supplied with what he desires."

"If no individual's good enough, why don't they use a team of cooks then?"

"They say he claims he has yet to find one cook who can prepare for him a perfect meal—no sir, not even a perfect dish, they say."

"With the exception perhaps, of the maid?"

"Man can't live on that all the time," the guard leered. "It ain't enough nourishment, sir!"

"Wouldn't one want to really try, now?"

"But not the king!" The guard laughed. "The old bastard's much too old for that sort of tenderness, if you know what I mean, sir. Save it for us younger men!"

"Well," I replied, patting him on the shoulder, "be sure to save some for me."

. . . he's in a bad mood . . .

"Aye, sir! Good night, sir! Oh, enjoy the stars, sir!"

. . . a bad mood . . .

"Good watch to you, soldier!"


They say that it is rare that a star is blocked by cloud here anymore.

The guard on watch in the dome beside me— There is nothing here within my radiation suit, I can shut off the radio, I can shut off the life support— No, that I leave in automatic operation; so quiet . . .

I remember clouds here. Vast acres of clouds—gigantic volumes, I remember them. The change in climate has been so drastic.

Oh, doesn't it seem odd that no one can stand outside the shielded glass of this dome, naked to the effects of the atmosphere?

Röntgen 5 to 15.

There are no more sounds of surface traffic, no more lewd pulsations if they were ever lewd at all—only the cries to the open mind of a below-ground stream of man.

Röntgen 5 to 15.

I wonder where the buzzards go at night. They tell me, to the ruins to the south. To patrol there, and then to sleep in the remains of the rubble—where, Woodward Street?

Probably.

And they say the new sounds of life, or those that survived, can be heard on the surface—they push their buried microphones up for electronic transmission, no radioactivity, they hear—they turn up their ears.

These natural sounds, are they now exotica?
But to me
Memories.


. . . But I shouldn't say "we" to myself. I was gone at the
time; about one light-year away if history is permitted to
stand correctly.

One light-year should separate me from the guilty—I was
way past the orbit of Pluto, I was far, far gone.

And yet, if there be a Creator—although I have found
evidence of none—if He exists, all human terms to Him are
worthy of a Holy laugh.

I'm actually shivering like the prince.

Oh, for the three hours I was protected enough.

I was cheated most horribly in that forest.

The scattered brick in the underbrush, sod over the
asphalt or what remained of it—still some traces of carbon-
ization.

Concrete. The shadow of a man caught upon a sidewalk
—fallen with his finger upraised.

A woman's skeleton, identified by the long hair that somehow was still stuck to the skull.

The Republic's vehicle waited for me at the absolute edge
of the forest.

There was a car all covered with rust; three people were
in it. Some of the flesh had mummified. Some of the clothes
had not rotted away.

Three hundred miles out, in the stars—ten months away:
the *Stellar*. The interstellar part of her anyway. An empty
collection of fuel tanks, shutdown M/C engines, a dead reactor, useless controls.

Falling.

She's set to tear herself apart when her orbit finally decays and she strikes the hardening edges of the air.

In the deep black damp of space—she's like a proper woman. All covered with the glowing gems of her stupid personality.

I thought myself to be in a most total Hell. I had a ten
percent chance of suicide—what good in faith is my journey
now?

Now I desire to pray to a Lord that I doubt exists,
though I made good pretenses.

One hundred and thirty-two years; all compiled in a batch
of paper and microfilm and tape—one vast computer program.

Perhaps in another hundred years some monk will

find it while searching for a means to confirm his God's existence, and then will throw the damned message away.

The King.

The King.

I'd best stop talking to myself.

The King and his motivation to use me eventually as a spy on his son, though now's too early for him to build the breach. It's too obvious a play of innocent personalities; it's clean, too. He believes that he can drag information from me concerning the sanity and affairs of his son by culture shock, intimidation after he gives me a yawning taste of the court —make me a big man in a month, then tear me down in a subtle way to the base core of nothing. And all because of my ignorance of the Republic's society; one false move on my part and because of my entrance, I shall be condemned.

This will all happen if what Brother Conrad told me tonight is true.

Why did he, not knowing me, come to me with this information that has stopped my sleep?

Why did he not tell the prince—he's his confessor.

That Wayne desires to succeed the King in power by declaring his son insane, and then after the King's death formulate a proxy government?

The night.

The world's night.

Whose side will be chosen tonight?

And the quiet wash of the wind that no one hears anymore.

Pity.

Pity.


". . . And did not the prince seem ill?" the Archbishop demanded forcefully.

"No."

I found him in my apartment living room. How he had found entry, I didn't know. I supposed it was his right.

"I don't know what you're talking about," I said.

Wayne, dressed in his ceremonial robes, confronted me like a massive gilded wall. His eyes were piercing. I'm certain he knew the watch schedules; he was that sort of a man. It was eleven o'clock, twenty-three hours, the mating hour, and so I would have expected him to be elsewhere.

"I simply asked," he crisply explained, "did the prince show any signs of any sort of disorder?"

"He did not this evening or day."

"Mental?"

"He seems more rational than any man I've spoken with, Father."

"We are concerned," he muttered softly, perhaps a little slurred, as if to draw me closer.

"We all are, Father," I said once, turning, walking quite around him, entering my bedroom, closing the door.

He's in a bad mood.
The meat must hide the taste of it.

In the morning I found a notice on my door for me to see the King at one P.M., thirteen hours, on Level 1, in the Republic's new construction wing.
Beyond the full protection . . .

# V

———◆———

Warm wind. . . . if I remember correctly, it was definitely . . . summer.

The last summer.

To the touch cold yet moist, but not refreshing—she was always the cold one, like snow.

This will crack her crystal heart, I thought.

There's always a woman left behind, even if she's just a memory tucked back somewhere within the celebral depths. She was the kind of woman who demanded to be hated so that she could in a superior way . . . love.

"I've got to go; it's the culmination of all my training!"

"James," she said in a maternal tone. "I don't see why you have to go to all this trouble. We have money; what more do you need?"

"Pride."

"Inflated egotism?"

"Hope."

"Childish, immature, spaceman's dreams, darling?"

"Don't be an ass, Mary; I'm going."

She looked up at the ocean as if pious in my memory, and we were still on that beach, still together in a mere physical world—still flesh enlocked. . . .

"Or is it that you're finished with me?" she said. "I have served my purpose in the education of one James Nathan Williamson—my money and my time, my body, my life?"

"I never touched the abundance."

"Why must you use people, James?"

"I . . ."

"Why must you keep only that which benefits you, then throw the rest away?"

"I . . ."

"Oh, stay with me, James. Take care of me."

"Perhaps," I replied, turning away, "I am the cancer of others' souls."


"Coffee, sir?"

42

. . . james . . .

An electronic pulsation.
A wire twitch somewhere—a noticeable twitch only to a voltmeter.

. . . take care of me . . .

Alerted, a series of relays threw; some metal warmed up but under the design tolerances. There was a nanosecond buzz. A capacitor fired. A series of new signals were sent. A rather stupid progeny of a computer glanced at these with a waking pseudo-eye, then diverted them down the proper wire pathways. A rat, walking along a coppery plate where he shouldn't have been, was suddenly electrocuted, and fell down twitching—now dead.

"Coffee, sir?"

. . . the cancer . . .

A series of motors, massive ones, opened up the panels to the sky—two steel underbraced, steel and concrete-sand-covered doors—because a blast shield had slid back. An hydraulic lift received air. It pistoned up, directing a folded-up object straight into the silent sunlight of now dawn.

. . . but did I love you, james?

"Coffee, sir?"

A lizard, rather sluggish this early in the morning, blinked lidlessly at the rising object, then scampered. A buzzard high up an air current spotted this movement, decided it was living, fled to higher skies.

. . . yet my imperfection . . .

The object unfolded with a bang! A light flashed on a Tri-Scann board. A captain on watch looked dully at it for a moment; pressed another button which gave a flash of light when activated.
A new series of electronic commands were dispatched.
At the fastest speed . . .

"Coffee, sir?"

don't leave me, james
don't leave me, james
don't leave me, james


"Program Eight, 'Scann activated, sir!"

"Coffee, sir?"

"What?"

The lieutenant smiled. He appeared to have been standing for quite a while, but the cup he held in his hand was still steaming as if freshly poured.

"Oh," I said, shaking my head, getting awake again, "thank you."

"You're welcome, sir," he said, giving me the cup.

"What's your name again? I don't think we've met before."

"George," he said. "George Kennedy."

"After the Cape?"

There was a silence between us.

"Cape, sir?" he said, arching an eyebrow.

"Just a place I used to know," I said slowly.

"Oh." He gave a short laugh. "Yes, sir."

"Thank you again. Back to your post, Kennedy."

"Yes, sir."


Sipping the hot black artificial drink, I activated with my free hand a series of status reports to be flashed up by the Defense Computer on my personal computer monitor, or PCM. On the far wall, facing all men—perhaps set up to create a great impression on the Military's visitors—a 360° Tri-Scann image was projected. It was essentially a long-distance (three hundred-mile), electronic overhead view of the area surrounding the Republic, covering altitudes from two hundred to one hundred and fifty thousand feet. There was a five-mile expanded view of the Republic's immediate area in the center of it. It was projected over a map. The expanded view indicated quite properly the flight plans of nearby buzzards that this morning were flying out and about —their weight, air speed, course, and percentage of fissionable material was indicated beside each image of the bird in electronic yellow.

Of course, a twenty-one-foot by eighteen-foot high screen was not necessary to do this on—twenty-three inches diagonally would have been more than enough.

The enemy just had to load down his fusion bombs with enough of the heavy elements; enough, the bomb carefully wrapped, to carefully lay down a radioactive base with fallout that would take the Earth five hundred years to erase.

And soon, no doubt, they'd finally solve the gigantic weight problem behind matter conversion weaponry type bombs, so the world wouldn't be an eraser anymore. . . .

PCM
a notice, flashing

"All stations," I said, shifting a bit in my command chair. "Standby for oh-eight-hundred check down."

Then two minutes later: "Commence check down."

observation-ground systems, Roger
weapons system, four, Roger
detection-electronic, Roger
damage control systems, Roger
defense computer operations, Roger

"Kennedy?"

emergency communications, Roger

"Yes, sir?"

weapons systems, three and one, Roger

"Good coffee."

medic evac, Roger

"Thank you, sir."

weapons system, two, Roger

"Friedreich?"

power system one, Roger

"Yes, sir?" said the general operations officer.

power system two, Roger

"Do you have the time?"

life support, Roger

emergency life support, Roger

"Why, it's oh-eight-hundred, sir. Eight hours, sir."

military standby, Roger

"Oh, so it is, isn't it?"

emergency lighting, Roger

"Sir?"

civilian defense, Roger

"Never mind."

Faces, we all thought.
· We saw faces in the cars and on the streets within the schools from the bus and from the sidewalk . . . day . . .
We saw them pressed in granite concrete bronze and sometimes gold, these images, illusions . . .

. . . illusions . . .

"Defense Command," a sterile voice chanted with a perfection of cadence.
An electronic voice had made the chant.

. . . illusions . . .

The voice had come over a loudspeaker which was mounted over the emergency exit hatch—the hatch itself was mounted in the rear bulkhead of Defense Command.
Not from the loudspeaker mounted over the normal entrance, the closed elevator doors.
Level 15 was where the emergency hatch led. Sealed off, guarded, empty Level 15.
I looked up from the last dot on my checklist, a final dot that I had confirmed with a light pen. "What?" I muttered, in reaction to it.

. . . illusions . . .

"Gentlemen: the prince."
At the hatch there was a click and then a spin of something. "Gentlemen," I said. "Bear in mind you're standing an

official watch: Stay completely on station with no formalities observed, as per regulations."

The chorus: "Yes, sir!"

... illusions ...

I wondered at the time whom the prince had bribed.

... illusions ...

He was dressed in a standard officer's uniform with no rank upon it.

... these images, illusions passing time ...

The station where I sat was mounted in the center of Defense Command, and separate from the control panels mounted on the walls. The station was set on a platform which rose two inches off the floor. It had a stainless steel railing at belly level which ran around the platform, enclosing all, with a gate that opened with a subsonic tone.

... time ...

His eyes were like friar's lanterns; they seemed to cast a flame about, a cold flame, bitter with its depth.

I glanced toward Friedreich and watched him hide comic books beneath his buttocks and then appear as if he knew his purpose here; or was that a preparation or a motion of action?

... time ...

Dreamlike, the prince clasped my shoulder in greeting, and that forced my eyes to turn with the rotation of my head in acknowledgment to that clasp.

... time ...

A shiver ran through the gamut of my body with the forces of our positions: Caught.

... religion ...

It was only the shading, the background, the atmosphere? "Your highness," I said with no emotion, with a neutral

tone, my eyes looking up to study his face for a minute,
then down into my work.

Display: Electrical Power Production (EPP), Load; Demand, Power System 1, Commercial Grid.

Thermocouple Bank A, three reactor-generator plants in
seventy-five percent operation. Thermocouple Bank B in closed
mode. One reactor-generator plant off the line in reserve.

. . . religion . . .

I switched to a display of surface weather conditions
and . . .

"Good, good James," he said in a hoarse voice. "Efficient
James."

*Eighty-seven* degrees Fahrenheit; eighty-seven. Humidity
at ten percent . . .

"The same, your highness," I said.

. . . religion with a divinity of god . . .

"Your men," the prince said, his voice wavering. "They
seem to ignore me. Am I a ghost already? Why?"

"Because, my lord," I said, while switching off the weather
display, "they are to remain at their posts at all costs and
observe no formalities; it is so dictated by the King."

The prince laughed.

. . . for caught in our emotion . . .

"You mean," he cried, "I'm stumbling across my father's
work?"

"More his proxy lordship, my lord, this rule being made
by some obscure general long ago and approved by the king
of his time, then passed on with the succession."

"I see," he said, his laughter over, now draping his arms
on the stainless railing. "Then there's no humor in it."

I turned away, listening to voices in my ears passed for
miles by electrons. . . .

. . . emotion . . .

"Indeed, James, I always thought that the backside of
your head possessed a set of eyes," the prince said.

"They're brown, my lord," I muttered aloud.

"Prove it."

"Roger, OB four," I said into the microphone taped to my

neck. "You are clear and the emergency relief change is so noted. Retire to the nearest infirmary for assistance and file a status report. To the emergency relief: the orders of the day can be obtained by the code CS five-three-oh-nine-one, Defense Computer."

. . . emotion . . .

"My father's ill," the prince said. "Because of that illness, I am denied his presence, and yet at this very minute, sickness and all, that man's reviewing the construction firmly occurring on the first level."

I looked up. "Oh, the guard?" I said. "Flu, probably; it's been around."

The prince slammed his fist on the railing. "Damn my father!" he said forcefully but without intent.

. . . we are struck before the wind . . .

"Treason can be assigned to princes, my lord," I said softly.

"Am I not man enough to be heard?"

"With reason, yes. With malice, no man has a chance."

. . . like leaves we scatter . . .

"What is your purpose, your majesty?" I said.

"Purpose?"

"What do you want of me?"

"Friendship."

"That I give you—but what do you desire here?"

The prince shook his head.

"I," he began in a halting way, "I . . . wish a view . . . of the surface, James."

"The surface . . ."

. . . like leaves we scatter
gilded
bronzed
or stoned . . .

"They don't let princes outside this place in radiation equipment." The prince laughed. "Not even up in the observation posts!"

And then, a moment later . . .

"Don't you understand, James? He may have his royal testicles, those precious little organs, damaged!"

. . . so we gape and stare at statues . . .

"James!" he cried, shaking my shoulder.
I looked up at the prince. "If it's a view you want, your majesty," I said, "it will only take a minute."
"Efficient James," he said.

. . . stare . . .

"Kennedy!"
"Yes, sir?"
"Transfer the Tri-Scann general readout to one of your monitors."
"Yes, sir."
"Richkart!"
"Sir?"
"Deploy surface camera A and project its image on the main screen for his majesty."
"Yes, sir!"
"Here we go, my lord," I said, looking up to him with a smile, but he was caught with the flickering of dead signals on the main screen, his fixed eyes waiting for the camera's observations.

. . . stare at statues
with the snow draped cross their heads . . .

A tower shot up from the concrete surface mound all shiny and chromed in the golden sun.

. . . heads . . .

A camera lens twirled with a slight buzzing sound which didn't fit its function, a buzz instead of a whirl—f-stops expanding; light gathering.

. . . heads . . .

. . . the sounds of a city full with population, engorged with automobiles and other effects of that population; the sounds of life baked on hot black pavement, burning . . .

. . . heads . . .

. . . children playing baseball in a city park and the garbage men slugging the gut of their work into the womb of a battered turbine truck to be packed, hauled, and recycled away . . .

. . . we see the vacuum there . . .

. . . little girl looks up from first base: oh, mom, look up at all the silver planes up way up in the air; all those pretty white streaks . . .
. . . flower opens and sun comes out to blot the sun; the little boys begin to burn and the great garbage turbine goes slam-bang! falls on its side, and like metallic tinkertoys bits and pieces fall apart and the potato peels crisp with black while spinning in midair . . .

. . . and we lift our eyes and see the stars . . .

"My father," the prince whispered. "Oh, what strange distortion is this?"
"There's not much to see; shall we pan three hundred and sixty degrees?"
"There's more than one location for Hell."
"And paradise?"
"There's more than one location for that, too."
"And . . ."
Down for a moment of silence.
Down for a second of nonanimation and all things at full stop.
Down for an hour of eternity.
Drink.

"Sir!"

## WARNING

"Target bearing two-four-seven point oh-seven-one!" Kennedy bent closer to his screen. "Altitude at two thousand steady. Speed: Mach one point seven. Attack Zone Time Arrival: Mark, five minutes. Designation: Manned aircraft, heavy bomber. Percent fissionables: eight point nine percent."
"Stay put, my prince," I said quietly, touching his arm.

## WARNING

He raised his eyebrows in a form of shock. "James?" he said.

"Condition Red," I said.

RED

Every military installation hatch slammed shut and locked, sealing all at their defensive stations, save the observation crews.

RED

"Observation Guards to shelters," I said. "System four, are you tracking?"

"Roger."

"Compute firing solutions. You are go for firing at my command."

"Yes, sir."

"Friedreich," I automatically called, my training now in effect. "Safeties are off on all survival/blast systems and all weaponry systems. Carpman, standby for auto/activation of M/C cannon within the short and middle systems. Talbert, standby for system one, the long system."

RED

Electronic stimulations.

RED

Numbers danced up from the Defense Computer, were caught by eyes, and then spun back down to the computer again.

RED

"The King," the prince said softly.

"Kennedy," I said, "switch your general image plot back to the main screen. Jones, retract that damn camera. Standby for evacuation analysis."

RED

There was a sputter of photons, and the Tri-Scann picture came back to life before us.

It was there at the extreme of the Tri-Scann's altitude

sensitivity, about one hundred and twenty miles away and closing fast. Although the Defense Computer's calculations could not be accurate due to poor signal quality—still, it looked like a seventy- or eighty-megaton payload.

RED

"Damn, damn, damn," Friedreich said. "Nothing in the air, and we don't have enough time to scramble anything."

RED

"Evacuation status?"

"Mark," cried Kennedy. "Four minutes."

"Negative," Jones replied. "We're beginning the nine hours' shift change. Computer indicates negative for location of population to below Level ten, negative to corridor drill because we can't muster enough wardens."

"The King," the prince muttered.

"All right," I said softly. "We're ready here. Friedreich— get the Level one detachment to the construction area—the King's there! Get him to the royal shelters."

RED

Saying nothing, the prince moved up to the main screen and put his hands behind his back and studied the approaching plane.

RED

I found myself intently watching the prince's shoulders; there was a slight shaking to them.

RED

"Sir!" cried Jones. "Emergency Power systems are now in total operation, we are approaching . . . Mark! one hundred percent power capability!"

RED

Almost in a whisper, so soft was the voice from the missile bank.

"Solution," the man five miles away said.

"Fire as per program," was my immediate answer.

10

Now, the prince stood too stiffly.

9

I got up from the command console, taking my eyes off the prince, and walked the three paces to Kennedy's station.

"Three minutes until target's in cannon range," he said softly.

8

"Talbert," I said. "Get system one, the long to the surface, test and track target. Standby all other systems which have not yet been ordered to fire."

7

This was the time when the fear came up and mocked.

6

"They're having difficulty finding the King," Friedreich said.

"What?" the prince said sharply, turning from the screen.

5

"Do not be alarmed, my lord," Friedreich said. "There's still time."

"Yes," he said hoarsely. "We have time, don't we? Plenty of time. Time. Time."

4

I patted Kennedy on his shoulder once, and started for the prince.

3

The foot came off the floor and the leg behind pushed upward, then the foot came back down.

2

The prince glanced at my coming; his eyes closed once and he bent his head to the right and turned his silent back to me.

"Destiny," he then said.

**1**

"Are you in distress?" I asked, touching his right arm.

"Stay away," he said softly. "Else the infection may pass to you."

**"SYSTEMS A & B, MISSILES 1 THROUGH 18 FIRED"**
the                    gave            buzz of
        computer           a slight             ecstacy

In the mind they could be seen springing from their launchers, inflamed by their exhaust. They, the anti-aircraft missiles, sprang up on the Tri-Scann screen as bright green dots that left pale, fine green streaks as they made their way to their target.

"Infection?"

"You know the disease, James."

"But I . . ."

"And they're out to remove me, James—we both know our sources. . . . Are you one of them, too?"

"Am I in that position?"

"Does it require circumstance to render a decision of action?"

"I . . ."

"Have you no ideals?" Then he started to move away. "They're using you, James. This entire social order—you're a pawn because you have made no choices. But, ah, these anti-aircraft missiles, what fine vehicles they are employed in the defense of the Republic. They're machines after the bull's-eye. And we are damned. The devil's machines, they are. We are damned, James, because like the fools in the past we have nothing worthy of salvation. Is all of this waste? We too are that same bull's-eye—it matters not what weapon is employed or who employs it. My father . . . my pitiful poor father induced to actions by others by a poverty of the soul. Can you understand that, friend?"

"This is not the time for understanding."

"No word of the King, yet," said Friedreich, and then he went to other things.

"No word of the King," echoed the prince. "Is he lost in

the construction in there? Can't he sense the danger? To shelter he must go. To shelter. Oh, I am trapped in a sea of no word, but then the words are of no value. Do we have any standards anymore? Did we ever? Is everything machine-like? Are commercial salvation and resurrection objects to be paid for only in precious fine material things? My father. Give me my father. Give me flesh; humanity! That's the only stuff of value!"

"My prince!"

"My father!" he cried, running toward the locked exit hatch from whence he had come. "I must go to my father!"

. . . missiles approaching target area, kennedy in a dream read . . .

"You shall not leave here, my lord."

"The hatch, James?" he cried.

"Locked by our condition, my lord."

From his uniform he whipped out a small laser pistol. "There's little time," he said slowly. "Unlock it, James —you have the key. Let me go free to catch my father."

"A king's command as old as the Republic bids me to keep you here, my lord," I said calmly. "A laser will not help. There's safety here. You are the successor to the throne, and, Robert—they'll find the King, don't worry."

"They save nothing!" the prince screamed, turning his pistol on me.

I moved a step forward. "Why must you go?" I cried. "To watch your father die with you? Is that destiny?"

He raised his gun to the ceiling, his hand tightly clenched around the grip and his face silverplated with sweat. "We are not worthy!"

I lunged forward, knocking him and pistol against the hatch. Away forward the laser spun. We separated, and he went for the gun. I grabbed him and slammed him against a fire extinguisher. He kicked me in the abdomen. I fell back. He hit me full in the jaw as I got up, knocking me down very hard. He pounced for me on the floor. I rolled away. We were separate and on our feet. I hit him with a right into his face, and he ducked down and I got a knee to his groin, but he came back with a right into my stomach, knocking me away to the floor.

Friedreich got him with a clean stun and the prince collasped.

"Thanks," I said, looking up at him as he picked up the prince's laser pistol and handed it to me.

"For what?" Friedreich replied, breaking out into a smile. "We all must do our part."

"Remind me to buy you a beer."

"Sir!" cried Kennedy. "System's missiles are being deflected!"

I walked over to his station and saw them falling away from the bomber's Tri-Scann blip like stones being tossed on earthen ground.

"Dammit," Friedreich said over my shoulder.

"Look at that," I said, pointing to the computer figures on the screen. "High intensity flux field screwing up our guidance; if he can project that he can shield single M/C blasts. Too bad we can't determine polarity."

"So what?" said Friedreich. "We hit him with a salvo!" Kennedy and I both looked up in awe.

"Did I say something?" Friedreich cried, backing away slightly.

"Get to your station and check out with the Defense Computer a double power massed shot with system one, maximum range minus one half mile inclusive, with a five percent dispersal."

"Gotcha!"

I pounded Kennedy's back. "How much time until cannon range?" I asked.

"Sixty-four seconds," he replied, tightening the Tri-Scann focus.

"Sir," Jones called, looking over from his station. "We have power plant seven reactor, demanding a power down."

"Negative," I said, shaking my head. "Let them stay in the yellow—but keep them on emergency damp readiness status."

"Roger."

"Jesus Christ!" Friedreich cried. "It's on the money—we'll give him an anti-photon wall to climb, the filthy bastard!"

. . . with pitiful screams the lizards
flew through the screaming air
and the dust came up . . .

The cannons blew up on their mounts.

. . . the glassite of the observation domes disappeared
there was a big wind . . .
. . . the blast shields rocked, the safeties fired; the
blast roof of every level quaked on its coils in ecstacy . . .

... the King looked up and saw a massive new ...
... all the people ...
... they fell down ... .

And the prince on the metal deck was silent to the world, unattended.

... while ...

Five lizards stood on their four haunches each and watched from different directions the cannons swiveling on their mounts.

". . . estimate on warhead still good at eighty megatons . . ."

a steady
   stream of steam cooked
     carrots

   Six robot dolls

... while ...

. . . is it really alive, james? Are we but the bastards of a Creator, cast aside down from greatness, alone to fend only for our pitiful selves?

FIRE

   "All cannon long system fired!"
   "Kennedy, did he divert?"
   "Sir . . . he has prematurely deton . . ."

# PART 2

# Realities

## VI

They gather in the holy central church, the Church of the Just. Their feet echo off the plastic imitation granite, their whispers reverberate off the plastic walnut paneling. The stereovision cameras zero in. Thousands more are watching and tuning their stereovision sets in. The priest checks his makeup for any flaws, the final check, moves out of his room, mounts the steps of the altar. The priest displays a gold-colored cross to the cameras, and then to all. The twenty handpicked worshipers kneel on the special pads that are set within the floor before the altar. A monk approaches the lectern; murmuring prayers, he opens the sacred book.

Thus the mass begins.

Electronic unison—the songs are sung, the paper prayers are chanted, the body crosses are made.

The electronic equivalent of a pipe organ built in 1600 A.D. plays.

The lights dim, expand, die down for the glorification.

The burning candles flutter in a fake, unnecessary breeze. . . .

" '. . . And there appeared to me,' " the priest read, his voice amplified and seen on a VU meter as a series of throbs of the needle—the external part of that voice falling on the actors surrounding him, " '. . . a great golden throne, and One who seated upon it made both the sky and earth flee and vanish.' "

"Amen," the actors cried on cue.

" 'And His Spirit fell upon the leaders of this past nation and all knelt before Him for they knew and feared His Wrath.' "

"Amen," the actors cried, their united voices trailing off in the reverberator's spring units.

" 'And I heard a great voice,' " the priest read passionately, " 'from that throne cry out: *The home of God shall be with men, and God shall live among them, and they shall be His people, and God shall wipe the tears from their eyes.*' "

"Amen," the voices chanted.

" 'And then the voice commanded,' " read the priest: " '*Build great underground temples from which those that are to be saved from the first fires of purification shall dwell in happiness in My Name!*' "

"Praise be to God!" the actors' voices rang.

" 'These that shall survive shall worship God, they shall see His face, and on His privileged servants the sign of Jesus shall be written upon their foreheads. Night shall be no more, neither shall day; they will have no need for sunlight for the Lord God will watch o'er them.' "

"Praise be to God!"

" 'Yea, though this will come to pass, I say beware! For the forces of Satan will follow thy example, and will cast their false Gods upon the earth in search of rape.' "

"Amen," the actors called back, their voices now lowering as per cue in volume.

" 'Shut out from thy temples the depraved, the sorcerers, the impure, the idolators, the murderers, and all that practice and do love a lie!' "

"Amen."

" 'For I am the Alpha and the Omega, the first and the last, the beginning and the end, One that was and One that will be, and the time of My Kingdom is near.' "

"Confess," the blinding light said.

"Go to Hell!"

No, it came from a man, that word: "Confess."

I came back to the world strapped on a table, a table quite hard on the back. It was metallic and cold and hard and I lay flat on it, with my wrists and ankles bound apart.

The hand came up and around and down and across—my cheek felt its imprint.

"Confess," said the monk, dressed in gray robes, with a vial of holy oil in his left, quiet hand.

They had sedated me with a laser stun as I got off watch,

arrested me apparently, stripped me, and brought me to wake up bound nude on a metal cold table.

There were electrodes set on my skull and held in place by tape.

Surrounding me in hum, there was the sensory evidence of electronic equipment.

"Confess," said the monk.

Yes, it was the overhead light, wasn't it? Intentionally vision-defeating, made even more so by the absolute white walls, the pale monk's face, the polish of the table—even the crucifix on the wall in front of my feet was made of some white, artificial substance. Someone had taken the time to hand-paint in the red marks of Christ's tortured blood.

"Confess," said the monk, yawning.

"Screw all of you," I said. "Damn lousy way to wake up. Confession? Confession. All right, I am a most horrible man."

The monk looked up toward the ceiling where I couldn't turn my eyes because of lighting conditions.

"Confess," he whispered. "For your soul's good."

Another man stood by, whitened to death in the harsh light, his chest bare, a black hood on his head, and he held a whip that was black and shiny in the wash.

"Confess," said the monk.

Another man was by the hooded man; he too wore a hood, but he held a club that was made of wood.

"Confess," said the monk.

I could hear the fourth man behind my head. He was switching dials and tabs about on an equipment control panel, producing an abundance of ultrasonic hums as he set devices into their proper integrated operations.

"Confess," said the monk.

I laughed. "Confess?" I said. "What the hell for? I haven't paid my donation. I haven't received my ticket. Is there a wafer waiting for me, somewhere?"

"Confess," said the monk.

"What is this taped to my skull? Electrodes? A bit of improvement to the human nervous system? Spike up the old neurons a bit?"

"Confess," said the monk.

I coughed. My chest heaved with it. The sound of that cough reverberated over the sterile white tile walls, through the men, over the white tile floor, within the metal table, about the crucifix hanging. It registered as a fluxion of electronics within the humming equipment.

"May God forgive your silence," the monk said, lifting his

hands as a signal for the technician to turn the potentiometers up.

"I am not the silent one, monk," I replied.

The men all paused for a moment. Perhaps they were waiting for the effect. Without any calling from the monk, they soon began to work their honorable trade upon me.

The electronics amplified the pain to a high degree.

The whip flew through the air.

The flesh began to darken and weaken from it.

The bones vibrated to the sonics of the club.

Only black unconsciousness brought relief from it.

4.79 Mev
4.05 Mev

#####rise in $Sr^{90}$ concentration, half life/ 25 years##### a Beta particle was formulated through the following equation:

$$n = p + e\text{-} + \bar{v}$$

. . . damage control . . .

"You didn't have to punish him so much!" she said.

BREACH
BREACH
BREACH

. . . bulkhead number one, level one is closed and sealed . . .
. . . it's the new construction area, there wasn't enough time to finish the blast shielding. . .
. . . the king is dead.
the king is dead.
the king is dead?
the king is dying.
oh, the king is dead . . .

"I need blood," she said. "Type A, Rh positive."

. . . heart, 120 . . .
. . . respiration warning . . .
. . . always a heavy bomb, sir, although this time the device was clean. No sodium or cobalt 60 jacket. It's puzzling, sir, that they kept it so. . .

"He could have been killed by you clods," she said.

". . . Well, the blast wave destroyed the safety circuits in the new development, whereas he was protected from the flash, he received a probable six thousand Röntgen dosage, besides his physical wounds."

". . . Casualties?"

"Thirty-five killed in the cave-in, about a hundred and twenty wounded, and they are receiving last rites."

... let him go
it's the radiation
let him go
it's the radiation
let him go ...

". . . It's the radiation," I apparently said.

"He's coming around," said the woman's voice which drifted over my head. "We don't have to thank you about that."

"We all have our duties to perform," said the monk. "Whereas our subjects are the same, the departments are not. Make him alive."

"Survived," I said. "Survived."

"What's he muttering?" the monk asked. "There's no sense to it."

"You're in my way," the woman said.

... beware of secondary ground shocks, said a man...
... emergency power sustained, said Kennedy ...

"What a way to survive," Friedreich cried, shaking his head while his face was awash in the red alarm lights. "What a miserable way to survive."

... death to the king
the king is dying
the king is dead.
what a miserable way to survive
what a miserable way to die ...

". . . Survive," I said. "Survive."

"That's the message," the woman said. "That's what you're doing, darling."

She was swabbing something that burned on my back.

"What?" I said in a stupor, rubbing my chin as I twisted my head to the side on the sheet that was taut on the examination table.

"You've come back to life," she said, waving some sort

of electronic device about one inch above my back. "How do you feel, handsome?"

"Dead."

"You look it, too. Now hey! Don't you dare go on that back, big boy—you stay lying on your belly, do you understand?"

"All right," I said quietly.

"Hold tight while I plastic up your skin."

"Yes, ma'am."

"That's better, darling."

"What's your name?"

"Genevieve," she said, busy spraying a cool liquid over the wounds. "Genevieve Christian."

I tried to raise my left arm.

"You've suffered some temporary neural inhibitions, my dear," she said softly. "These will die away in a few minutes."

"What the hell happened?"

"Watch your language!"

"I'll put it in a better tongue, then, young lady. *What* have they *done* to me?"

"You've been beaten to a bloody pulp," she said in a neutral tone, moving away somewhere, "and they've given your body to me so that I can make it fit enough in an hour's time to stand trial."

"Oh."

"They did almost too good a job, those animals."

"I suppose I'm still undressed?"

"Huh? Oh, I've seen naked men before."

"Forgive my appearance, then," I said.

"What's there to forgive, James?"

"You know my name?"

"The entire Republic knows your name."

"Oh."

"Would you please turn over now?"

"Sure."

I almost blacked out, for my back flamed up in a most total pain.

"You're lucky," Genevieve said. "They didn't break any bones."

She was a brunette, but the rest of her was out of focus.

"How nice," I said through closed eyes. "Where are they now?"

"Oh, I chased Brother Redmund out of here a while ago —took me ages to convince him that you weren't going anywhere for a long time."

There was a press of something against my left arm. "Let's see what this will do for you," she said.

Now she leaned over me, and I could smell her perfume and the warm press of her body against mine as she opened one of my eyelids, flashed a light, and peered within.

"I believe I'm ill," I said.

She was pretty fast with the necessary apparatus. She wiped my mouth with a paper towel. She pushed my arms away as she gave me some water.

"Still got problems, huh?"

"Sure beats the flu."

I opened my eyes and blinked a few times and noticed that the image was coming into focus toward clarity now, and had stopped spinning.

"Think you can sit up?"

I discovered that I could do that without too much disoriented dizziness.

She started to massage my neck.

"Tell me," she said after a minute. "Did you really strike the prince?"

"Yes."

"Why?"

"To keep him safe from the attack."

"To keep him safe?"

"What he desired was martyrdom; he wanted to die with his father, if he could have found him."

In the silence that followed, the muscles of my body gradually stopped a type of spasmodic quivering and just throbbed in a stiff pain.

"Let me be quick," she said, talking softly in my ear. "I'm pretty certain that they haven't microphoned my office, but I'll play it clear. I'm sure you've talked to Brother Gates recently, haven't you, darling?"

"Concerning the Church? Yes."

"Brother Conrad Gates is at present organizing a church to replace the old."

"What?"

"Quiet, James," she said, leaning closer to me. "Don't strain yourself, not after what you've been through, love."

She was quite an attractive woman even in a doctor's smock, with great folds of sweet hair that softly caressed her shoulders and breasts.

"What concern am I to you?" I said. "I am a dead man."

She was serious. "James," she said. "You are my patient deliberately."

"I'd better be."

."Don't be bitter, my dear James, that's not proper of you."

"The rain must die," I said.

"No," she said, shaking her head.

"And the wind will fail and there will be nothing left to continue life, for we have left and let the surface go—we are beings without a word called love. We are beings of finality."

"I have to be quick, James."

"Call the monk in; let me go."

"Can't you understand?" she cried, shaking my shoulders. "I was put here to save your soul, dammit! Oh, you're impossible."

I looked up at her. "Madam," I said. "You can't save something that never existed."

There was a new silence of shock between us, a ventilator opened and released a stream of cooling air; my body seemed like a revived mass of flesh filled with sores and other bleedings here and there about.

"Look, mister," she said with nostrils flaring. "You and I both know the Church's Bible is not the correct Bible."

"Don't make fantasies with me, Genevieve," I said.

"Don't be a blockhead."

"It doesn't matter to me that the henchman believes in a holy book whose wording has been changed to support the theocracy in power—only his existence bothers me."

"Stop being an ass," she said.

"All right," I sighed, lifting my head up to the ceiling. "What troubles you?"

"I'm shocked!" she cried. "Brother Gates makes a discovery of this importance—you knew it all along—but then one man's not enough, so you're excused. But God, James—Wayne's Church is the Church of the Anti-Christ! It's a blasphemy! And that means nothing to you?"

There was a long moment as she studied me with an angered expression on her face, her eyebrows depressed, her lips set in a tight frown. But then that expression of sympathy was there, and colored by other things that for me were not as pleasant as human sympathy. They were for justice to the body in the grave—grief.

And her hair fell down on her shoulders to touch her finely-shaped breasts; all brown was that hair with a hint, in the office's garish light, of the luster pure sunlight could reveal if given the proper opportunity.

"Yes," I whispered, looking into my hands. "Somewhere that has a meaning."

"If only I hated you," she muttered.

"What?"

"Do you need proof, James?" she cried. "Well, we have found proof!"

With that, she went over to one of the white equipment cabinets in the corner of the room, shuffled some of the instruments around, and removed a familiar, small burgundy-colored book which she brought to me and placed in my hands.

The book had seen a passage of time, and the color of its binding was faded, and the lettering on the outside washed away, but the impressions made on the yellowed paper within were very clear:

### THE HOLY BIBLE
Containing the OLD and NEW TESTAMENTS
Translated out of the Original Tongues

Being the Version set forth A.D. 1611
compared with the most ancient authorities
and revised: A.D. 2006-2009

Newly Edited by the American Biblical Revision
Committee New York A.D. 2011

"The age has been confirmed by test," she said.

"Where did you find this?"

"Within the ventilation system. We found a box of fifty."

I started to laugh softly.

Genevieve bent down to look into my eyes.

"So," I said. "Now you need a martyr?"

# VII

They shoved me into what was either a total isolation cell or a dungeon to spend the night.

It was a dark dungeon, though the concrete floors were clean and very smooth. There was an elevated bench of concrete set against the wall so that one could sleep above the floor. There was a plastic light fixture mounted on the ceiling, and the light had been dimmed, but not so much that a hidden camera could not function. The fixture probably housed the microphone. There was a water fountain mounted on one wall, and a sort of ceramic basin underneath with the standard valve for sanitary functions.

It all made a very nice cage.

Its intention was to eventually break a human being's pride and reduce him to a more manageable primate.

On the wall opposite that which held the water fountain, there was a square crusty patch that looked like a piece of rough cloth which had been painted to resemble concrete. It probably hid the camera lens. The wall commanded a full view of the cell.

All of this I observed while sitting on the floor which sloped slightly to the center where there was a drain.

Only moments before they had thrown me in; something soft had been tossed in with me and had fallen on my protesting body. My naked skin had flinched against hard cold concrete. And then, the massive steel door had slammed shut behind me, the lock clicking into determined place.

The soft thing was soft *things*—one was my uniform, which had all its trimmings taken off and contained nothing of use for a potential murderer; the other was a pair of flannel pajamas with no fasteners other than a Velcro strip.

I smiled at the camera, waved, and put the pajamas on.

During the remainder of the night I did not sleep.

I had slept on concrete before, as a child. I could have slept, but something kept me awake.

It was the endless tread of the guard's feet on the floor of the corridor outside the cell, the corridor I had been dragged

68

down. But no, that couldn't be. The door was young steel and thick. It was a speaker mounted somewhere. It was a recording.

Yet, their leather-like soles made a brushing sound on the fine, thick-pile carpet laid there and their eyes were probably sedated by the fine luxury of the corridor's walls, luxury permitted to prisoners in brief glances, or hurried trips to the executioner.

Occasional glimpses of reality.

Reality in their book is a good room then, good clothing, and a fine warm bed on which to sleep.

The water was not made to be drunk. It was pure, but it was lukewarm, and it heated up to eighty degrees, and if you tried to plug the drain in order to flood the cell the faucet shut off automatically.

I spent the night thinking of myself, an admittedly selfish pastime, but one not dictated by choice.

My main thoughts were that I had never believed in Wayne's Church, and that my vows to him were lies, but then, I had never really desired religion. God was too nebulous to me. I needed an idol of substance.

My society was wrong.

And my society, at least in its beginnings, was founded on that same God.

They will come and drag me to Court. They will try me before their judges without a jury, for they are God's chosen men, and they will call me guilty of a fiction. That of the desecration of a prince. Then, they will excommunicate me, kill me, and toss me down the Big Fall. Perhaps my rebuilt atoms will form the substance of a shoe.

Why? The murder is politically motivated. Are they afraid of me?

I have excommunicated them.

How stupid men are.


The dying
            buzzard,
                    wings in motion,
                            glided down,
                                    turned,
                            spotted,
            then,

landed and perched on the still standing, semi-melted remains of one of the M/C cannon of the destroyed long system. It had been caught in the heat flash and blast wave, and rendered into total junk. The buzzard's coat of feathers had lost its shimmer. He would be dead very soon. Bits of drool slid carelessly from his beak. His mate had been killed; his survival was a miracle. There was plenty of carrion for him now, but he had lost his appetite. He perched and watched, his talons clenched about the steel and silicone mess; he watched the men in their bulky high-radiation suits driving their tank-like, atomic-powered vehicles around the surface mound, surveying the damage done to the surface installations of the Republic.

An antenna popped up out of the ground without warning and probed the skies for more enemies.

The surface observation posts had been blown away from the blast, their glassite bubbles broken, melted down, and fused to their bases. Men were now busy in the process of replacing them. The surface mound had survived, and the north, south, and east entrances were scorched but still usable. However, the west side entrance was jammed, welded into place, and would have to be blown off its mount for replacement. At the west southwest corner of the Republic, about one hundred yards outside the parameter where the barbed wire had been, there was a crater that was still exhaling smoke into the dark radioactive air.

The plane had detonated seven miles west, away.

Dust was still falling.

A camera popped up, looked at the buzzard, the buzzard peered at it for a moment, then the camera popped down below ground. The buzzard was tired, sick, not thinking too well.

There was a whirl somewhere the buzzard didn't notice.

A burned lizard was lying belly-up near the M/C cannon, just outside the battered upraised doors of the emplacement —outside the shaft that led underground. It had been protected slightly by the shadow of the doors. The buzzard examined it with some slight interest.

A barrel protruding from the surface mound started to center.

The buzzard looked up at the cloudy sky, flapped his wings slightly to gather the air about himself. It was unusually hot and perhaps the big black bird realized death was not far off. Perhaps he realized that he had never been this sick before.

Three .53 caliber detonating bullets entered the buzzard's body almost simultaneously from the machine gun and scattered the buzzard's remains, the tiny bits of bone and flesh and feather all over the ruin of the cannon, the blood seeping down the spoiled, fused erection apparatus, and dropping on part of the solid blast shield twenty-two feet into the underground.

Smoke wafted up from the protruding anti-personnel machine gun, and then the weapon was drawn back into its blast-protected compartment within the surface mound.

Feet had stopped.

I awoke from a daze not quite sleep or consciousness. It felt like morning. I picked myself up off the bench and then sat down on it, and watched the solid steel door which had no opening in it.

Feet had stopped.

There were keys turning in the lock. I would have thought they would have been more modern in that respect.

And then, at the point of inaudibility, I heard voices in the background; two guards arguing perhaps? But over what I could not be certain.

The dim night light in the cell happened to turn to full illumination without a sound, and one could feel the iris of the hidden camera responding to it. It was almost daylight in intensity. I could see now the slight traces of dust that had collected in the concrete corners.

The solid door opened.

A guard stepped in, looked about, and told me to get dressed.

"For what?"

"For trial."

I put on my bodystocking, the coat that once held the sash and rank, the boots, and then buckled the belt the guard handed me, leaving the pajamas on the concrete bench. My body groaned in its effort to comply with my brain's demand —it protested any action and all action. But at least part of me felt a semblance of normality, and I was certain that I wouldn't be suffering too long.

"Come on, you!" cried the guard who had first stepped in, moving into the cell and grabbing my arm, shoving a book into my coat opposite the camera, and then stopping to whisper very softly and quickly in my ear: "Don't worry, sir. Brother Gates understands.

"To trial!" he bellowed.

"To trial?" I said, while being dragged out. "So soon?"

The other guard grabbed my free arm. "We don't let traitors live long in the Republic!" he said.

# VIII

---

"So you admit that you actually struck the prince?" said Wayne from between folded hands.

Two priests surrounded the Archbishop at the table that was set before the altar of the Church of the Just, an altar which had a crucifix of Christ hung above it; there were no other people today other than myself, the monks of the Holy Guard (who grasped their swords in conviction), and the judges.

The hard, long, marble-like pews were empty.

Wayne's voice reverberated naturally in the large volume of the church.

Through the center doors of the sanctuary I was shoved, up the one hundred and seventy-five-foot aisle to the altar rail where I was permitted to say a prayer. The guard who had placed the book in my jacket shoved me down on my knees.

After a moment of silence, I was permitted to stand, and a priest read off my charges: that they had found me guilty of treason against the Republic, guilty of breaking my vows to the Church, and guilty of exercising the willful desire to do harm to an heir of the blessed throne.

I was asked to plead.

I pleaded innocent.

While they exchanged holy glances, I said that my orders bonded me to protect the holder of his throne and his heir from harm, that they made no stipulation concerning self-inflicted harm, that suicide was a sin, and that I had merely followed those commands.

"So you admit you actually struck the prince?" said Wayne.

"What is the evidence against me, Father?"

"The Court has seen the evidence."

"Do I not have the privilege of viewing the evidence?"

"In this matter—no."

"Father, beware the sin of Adam."

"Silence!"

72

"If it be **wrong** to stop a man's suicide," I said, "then I am truly guilty of that sin and do profess that guilt."

"No man has the right to strike royal flesh," Wayne countered.

"Why? Thou shalt not commit murder. Suicide is murder of self. Murder is mortal sin. Father, I merely stopped the prince from damning his soul."

"He merely wanted to find his father," Wayne argued back.

"His father was being searched for," I replied. "My orders are to make certain that the royal family is in an area of safety in case of an enemy attack. There is no safer place in the Republic than the Defense Command Center."

"The prisoner will be informed," Wayne said slowly, "that the prince is blessed by God, his birth is proof of it, and therefore can commit no sin. By the prisoner's own words he has confessed the crime of inflicting harm upon a member of the royal family."

"I inflicted no harm."

"Silence!"

"Neither did I commit treason or break my vows to God, Archbishop. My sin has been that of silence to this blasphemy."

The guards grabbed me. Those not involved with the action withdrew their laser pistols and looked up at the judges. Wayne sat back in his chair, his face sweating, and he ran his wet hands down his chest, flattening the robes there slightly.

"All right," he said. "Prove blasphemy."

"Proof?" I said calmly. "Perhaps, Wayne, it is right that you ask me for proof, for I had knowledge of the world before the accident happened. I knew God before what you call the first fires of purification occurred."

"It will do you no good to lie in a temple of God."

"Lie, Wayne? I need not lie; it is you who need to lie. There are people alive that know the truth, they have read the truth, they practice the truth behind closed doors, for if they brought it out you would crush it."

"The Anti-Christ," Wayne said softly to his priests.

"This entire fabrication is a lie, dear Archbishop. This Church has extensively rewritten God's work in order to make itself the *holy* one, its priests grow fat on bribes, and its Courts rule crime instead of redemption. Courts, dear Archbishop, corrupted by greed.

"I had knowledge of the true version of the New Testament, the Old Testament—I knew the Bible before I left for Bernard's Star. I have the knowledge that in your secret vault, Wayne, copies of it exist, copies that were confiscated during the establishment of the Church over a hundred years ago."

"Do you have more to say?"

"There is much more. That you are to murder me in order to prematurely release my venom before the damage is done—there are ears, here, Wayne. Who can you trust within this Church now? They may seem normal, but they may not be. And one final gift, Wayne—one present of farewell."

I held the Bible up for them to see. I tossed it into Wayne's lap.

"Where did you get this?" he cried.

"An angel gave it to me."

The guard took a monk's sword and struck my face with the hilt of it, knocking me to the ground. The skin of my cheek broke; the blood came down. The guard bent over me to drag me back up. "You've done your job well," I whispered.

"Anti-Christ!" Wayne screamed.

"Go ahead, Wayne," I answered. "It's a bloody trial; you didn't think I had anything to say, did you? Read that Bible. Sentence me to death to shut me up, though the message has been spread and with luck my death will only add validity. It was you who came to me and told me to observe the prince and report him mad; it was you who desired to convince the King of his son's insanity, to convince the King that the prince was unfit for the throne, and the time was ripe for the Church to rape it!"

"I am not on trial, here!"

"God is on trial. Wayne, though you may deny it—you are God."

"That's enough!" cried Wayne.

The guards grabbed me and silenced me.

Wayne looked around at the priests next to him and found that he was standing and they were sitting, and that they were staring off down the sanctuary somewhere.

"Gentlemen," he said. "I . . . I think the prisoner has proven his worth.

"You are to die in one hour," Wayne said to me. "Within that period, you shall be excommunicated from the Church. Return to Satan, friend. Your soul shall rot there."

I looked up at the guard.

The guard was silent.

Wayne looked up at the church's entrance. And then, the color began to fall out of his face.

"James!" cried the prince. "There you are!"

I turned and saw the prince advancing, his face all smiles and delight.

Wayne lowered his face.

The prince was dressed in a costume that was totally black, with a black mask dangling around his neck, and he wore a peaked black hat. Like an eager child, he grabbed a sword from the hands of a nearby monk, swung it happily in the air a couple of times, then came up to me.

"Where have you been, James?" the prince said, his voice exalted, vivid with energy. "I have been looking all about this marvelous place for you!"

The blood from my cheek was soaking my collar.

"I have been in jail, my lord," I said.

The prince screamed with laughter. "Oh, you weren't careful!" he cried. "Oh, James, James, you must take precautions with that serving maid; I hear she's as fertile as a cow!"

His laughter cut itself off in mid-breath.

He touched the blood running down my cheek with one hand.

"What sort of insult is this?" he said slowly. "Who did this to my friend? Who allowed this to happen to this man?"

"I have been charged with treason, my lord," I said, "and with the breaking of my vows to the Church, and with the crime of inflicting harm upon my lord."

The prince's eyes went from mine to the judges, to the monks, to the back of the church, to the crucifix on the lofted altar wall; then to Wayne's. In one fluid, quick motion he vaulted the altar rail, ran up, and stuck the point of the sword he carried against his Archbishop's neck.

"My lord," gasped Wayne, pressed against the back of his chair. "You do God wrong to display irrational violence in His church."

"You do me wrong, Archbishop," said the prince. "You spit on my black clothing; there's been too much murder here. The air, why, the very air's rotten with it. God's nose is wrinkling in disgust with it. Release James."

"Your highness!"

"He has committed no crime," the prince replied. "There will be no convictions while grief exists; we are bigger than low vengeance. It is a time for private weeping; let him go with your blessing."

"My blessing, my lord?"

"Bless him, Wayne!" the prince cried.

"Go!" the Archbishop gasped out, his face livid in it. "Go, James, and may the Spirit of God go with you."

"Amen," the prince added.

The thunder pounded the earth.

The wind, alive with the smell of the rape, flung its powerful body against all that stood in the way of its passage.

Massive drops of dust-coagulated rain slammed into the entrances facing the north, east, and south, flooded into the crater west. It coated the new construction; it made the melted remains of the damage slick to the touch.

"Rain," said the prince. "Thunderstorm."

They had removed the steel and lead shielding on the north door that had protected and hid the glassite panels placed there; the prince and I had given the guard an opportunity to take coffee. We were buried in radiation suits.

Pieces of debris, newly cracked again, were flung about by the wind.

What was left of the sick, burned animals struggled against the sudden transformation, huddled behind the ruins of the long defense system, boulders, under slabs of scorched upturned pavement; they lifted up their eyes.

The river would soon fill to the brim with the runoff of the plantless land, and its muddy carcass filled with drink would rush ever forward, ever swiftly and violently to its end.

"My prince," I said finally. "Are you mad?"

"Angered?" he answered whimsically. "No. Insane? Perhaps. I play at those games for political effect, James; the costume beneath this suit has no meaning. No, there is only one thing that I am."

"And that is?"

"A bastard."

"And so we all are."

"But I've received my confirmation."

"So have I."

"By what means?"

"Cain has been born; our religion has a foundation stone made from that."

"Yes." The prince laughed softly. "But my Adam died last night."

"My lord," I said. " 'Blessed is he,' they shall read when they crown you, 'who wears this crown, for he will lead God's saved, purified, and chosen ones on their road to eternity.' "

"How like tiny wars," the prince replied, "this thunder sounds. What a remarkable phenomenon, James."

"Yes, Robert."

"James," he said, turning to stare at me. "There are rumors that an invasion force has been dispatched from Chicago. Look to it. You are now Minister of Defense."

"But the Church, Robert. They would never . . ."

"To Hell with the Church!" he cried. "To utter Hell! For the Church blessed my birth, James—they made it legal over my dead mother's infertility. They allowed me to be."

He gave one last look at me, a brief glance, and departed.

And I was left with these thoughts: The thunder detonates. The wind takes revenge. The rain takes the job of making the skies clear again. The strontium decays. The radium decays. The by-products of all the bombs ever released to the world decays.

And the world decays.

# IX

One man's sleep ended quite normally at four hours, one minute, into the morning.

This singular man, as per habit, got up this particular morning and walked to his bathroom, a bathroom that was not counted as a room of his two-room apartment. There, he splashed some cool water over his gummed eyes and across the top of his bald skull.

The preprogrammed sleep center, malfunctioning slightly, although it was a quite useful rented device for men of his profession, now emitted a static click and the lights in the man's apartment went up to full intensity. Still, the sleep center had awakened this particular man at the proper time and continued to emit a subdued 10 Hertz subsonic tone which kept the man awake.

The mirror of the bathroom watched this particular man as he shaved, running a razor that didn't have a blade in its head but cut and sucked up the whiskers from his face efficiently, leaving only bare smooth skin behind; this device devoured the man's face.

The faucets of the sink before this particular man held his reflection as he washed, then electrically brushed his permanently coated teeth so that they would gleam properly. It tossed the reflection back as he proceeded to comb the limp gray remains of hair that circled his scalp like an ancient's wreath.

Checking the time, the nude man decided to wait about showering himself with soap and water until after work, and ran a chemical skin sterilizer over his clean body instead. The hand-held device emitted a slight mist. Bacteria were killed instantly.

This particular man drank a six-ounce glass of liquid for breakfast this particular day which contained within its liquid depth about three hundred and ten calories in various proteins and fats; that is, the drink.

At four hours, twenty-three minutes, the man was dressed.

He wore a simple green bodystocking with a black leather-

78

like belt and boots. He had a white protective helmet for his head, and wore on his chest a simple silver crucifix minus Christ on a silver link chain—this for decoration. On the belt he wore two pouches, one for the electronic tools of his trade, and the other for money, credit cards, computer matrix component files.

He touched the back of his left ear, for something hard was implanted underneath the skin there. Behind his right ear there was a similar device.

Slipping on a rather average-looking, silvery-colored ring, he began to hear monophonic sounds that seemed to be issuing directly into his left ear. He recognized the music as part of Ibert's *Escales*.

But he didn't want music today, he wanted the news, so he took out of a hidden pocket in his bodystocking a small key chain. Beside other things, one small thin hexagonal rod hung there. He found the proper, tiny, almost unnoticeable hole that was worked into the design of the ring, inserted the rod, and turned it until the proper station began to play.

. . . Funeral services for his late majesty Gregory will be conducted today at fourteen hours in the Hall of Kings, Level 7. The body will then be placed in state for the traditional thirty days of grief before recycled. The Archbishop of Wayne will conduct the Mass with a group of privileged citizens and royalty present. The entire proceedings will be stereocast at thirteen hours, fifty minutes . . .

. . . In other news, an equipment breakdown in power substation c, Level 12, caused a temporary halt to production on the Bairns electronics line, final assembly plant. The halt lasted twenty minutes and four seconds. The emergency generators of substation c immediately took over the life-support power load after what appeared to be a coil burnout occurred in the standard generators . . .

This particular man opened the door to his apartment, closed it, pressed his thumb on the print-sensitive lock to seal it thoroughly, and walked down the carpeted, deserted corridor of this particular residential section.

. . . Spokesmen say the coil burnout was caused by a sudden massive surge in power consumption. Repairmen are now checking the main service lines of power substation c for any possible breaks.

Power substation c, Level 12, supplies electrical power to the third or south quadrant of that particular level of the Republic . . .

The residential corridor emptied out into one of the main halls of the ninth level of the Republic. Two deserted pedestrian slide paths that ran down the center of it sped at five and ten miles per hour respectively. The paths were slick in their travels, the rotors beneath them well-lubricated, well-functioning.

As he left the residential corridor, the man turned to his right and walked five paces to a bike rack. He unlocked a three speed, red, twenty-six-inch bicycle which had cost him a cool two weeks' pay. He mounted it, backed off from the rack with his toes, then applied himself to the pedals and went away down the bike paths to the north, passing a man on a bicycle in the process.

"Probably one day there was a man who had written a lot of vaguely mathematical statements on a blackboard somewhere. Probably that man thought he could see some sense in them. So he tied a couple of the statements together, equated them with a couple of others, saw that everything looked good on his slide rule, and ended up with a fat check from his publisher who all along thought the man in question was a genius."

The man on the bicycle reached a curving ramp that led down to Levels 10, 11, 12, and 13. He braked and rode down to Level 12 in a tight spiral. The up-ramps were powered and had a high friction pavement to assist the bike rider; the down-ramps were not.

At his destination, this particular man exited, then turned east for about twenty yards, and stopped in front of the farm level's tiny chapel, one of the five that existed outside the one church of the Republic, the Church of the Just.

"Probably another man read the report of the first man, and decided that he too could see a hell of a lot of sense, particularly now in its digested state. So he, being more an applied scientist, built a testing device and proved the genius' big theory. And, of course, he ended up with two checks in his pocket, and the possibility of a fortune."

This particular man locked his bicycle in the small rack before the chapel, then from his wallet which he kept in a belt pouch he extracted two dollars.

". . . The testing device gathered dust for a while, in fact, perhaps it would have been forgotten. But then there came the great war. And people were stupid enough to believe that it was the final war. And with this war, there came the destruction of entire cities and populations. Millions of men were marching away and only thousands were returning. It was deadly to be a patriot.

"And fashionable.

"Another group of geniuses, perhaps motivated more out of fear than intellect, took the daring testing device and twisted it about a bit differently, then dropped the result on an entire enemy city.

"And then a second city.

"And the war was soon over.

"But the war wasn't won."


The hand of this particular man moved away from his ear while his other hand, his right, clutched the money. Down the Level 12 corridors, which surrounded the farms, there came the occasional sounds of someone going off to an early job, the huff-puff of the ventilators filling the air with subdued sound, and all the while the small machine before the chapel door hummed softly to itself.

He placed the two dollars in the tray of the waist-high machine, and waited about three seconds while a stereovision camera looked up to him. Then, the machine gave a buzz and issued forth a plastic receipt. Pocketing this, this particular man walked through the doors and sat down in one of the back pews.

Alone, this particular man was in the chapel.

On a stand next to the altar, encased in a red glass container, a single candle burned, the path of its consumption leaving a single upward trace of soot on the cream-colored wall.

This particular man bowed his head and folded his hands as if in prayer.

A cleaning robot, sensing the man's presence, hesitated at its closet door, then set itself on standby status with a silent electronic sigh. . . .

And then a monk, dressed in gray robes, entered through a door at the side of the altar, knelt for a moment, crossed himself, and walked over to the lectern that stood to the right of the crucifix hanging on the altar wall.

The monk opened the large book that lay on the lectern.

He crossed himself while doing so, and uttered a soft blessing over the text.

" '. . . And then He said to the gathering,' " the monk read,
" '*When you observe a cloud in the west rising, you say immediately that it is going to rain, and so it does. And when
you feel the south wind blowing up, flowing over you, you
say that it will soon be hot and so it happens. You fools! You
know how to interpret the feel of the earth and the atmosphere. Why can't you then figure out the meanings of the
times in which you live?*' "

"This be the word of God," chanted the monk, aloud.
"Amen," muttered this particular man.
". . . be the word of God."
"Amen . . ."
". . . the word of God. . . ."
"Amen . . ."

Nothing.
Thousand-foot long production lines of machinery, criss-
crossed with various conveyor belts, cranes, and the like,
kept eternally cleaned and polished by service robots—all
empty, empty; never used.
Gummed vinyl stickers set down by the men who as-
sembled the equipment one hundred and thirty-six years ago
still bore the clearly read inscriptions of blue and black and
red ink, and orange fine-tip marker.
Some inscriptions were simple checkmarks and/or X's in
proper boxes; others were more elaborate.
*OK'd by TH.*
*Good—WE.*
*Sys. 23C Check, Jim S.*
The floors were like new.
The original tiling was still in place, and it shone as if
made of precious well-kept metal.
This the particular man walked upon.
His ring was tuned to a different station now, and he
wore a collar around his neck which plugged into an antenna
that had been sewn in the right sleeve of his bodystocking.
He walked the corridors, humming.
It was five hours, twenty-two minutes.
He had taken something out of one of the two pouches on
his belt and had put it on his wrist, and that something dis-
played the fact that he was totally alone.
This particular man guarded particular production equip-
ment.
And there was nothing.
Nothing there.

Six hours, forty-one minutes.

Seven hours, eleven minutes.

This particular man ran his hand over the instrumentation boards performing the ritual hourly status checks of the equipment and observed that all was testing normally, that performance was assured, that everything was ready for the orders to be given.

Eight hours, thirty minutes.

This particular man took a coffee break with one of the guards who stood outside the specially locked doors to this section of Level 14, getting the coffee and bringing it to the guard from a small office near the guardpost, an office used for signing in for work and signing out.

Nine hours, even.

This particular man deliberated as to whether he should cheat a little and listen to an entertainment station on his radio, but decided that it was best he stayed tuned to the silent circuit that would give him his emergency orders, and keep him aware of the time on the hour.

Ten hours, eight minutes.

This particular man sat down on a small protective shelf on one of the nonrunning machines, and ran his hand over his face.

Eleven hours, twenty minutes.

This particular man yawned.

The escalator units to this enlightened section of Level 14 were sealed.

The elevators were locked.

The doors were closed, most locked, all guarded.

The life-support system here was cut down to minimum operation, for only one man really breathed the air here.

Even the lights were not maintained to their full brilliance, for only one man had to see with them.

The escalator units opened up and started running.

The massive elevators started to hum, and the panels over their doors lit up.

The locks on all the doors slammed open.

The life-support system started to whine, and seven giant blower units turned on, their blades spinning.

The lights opened up to full brilliance.

This particular man looked down the corridor of machinery in which he had frozen.

At the very end, a good eight hundred feet away, the green operating lights of the equipment flashed on. For a second, they waited at the very first bank of machinery, then in a flood moved on down toward this particular man in a sudden chattering of operations.

With a gasp the man started to run to the back.

The lights caught up with him, and passed him, and then all the machinery was operating.

With a loud clatter, the elevator doors opened, and a group of helmeted workers stepped off and headed toward their various assignments in the factory.

Men began to stream off the escalators and in through the doors.

"No!" this particular man cried as the first of the aircraft were incubated.

... won't he respond to the emergency recall?

"No!" this particular man screamed as the first of the radiation tanks were slammed together.

. . . come on, come on, harrison, stand back—stand back, will ya?

"No!" this particular man gasped as the rifles and pistols and rocket launchers and body armor were manufactured as if they were insignificant little things meant for a child's toybox.

... stand back! stand back!

"No!" he raged like a madman, pulling off workers from their stations who all fell to the floor, shrugged their shoulders, got up, and went back to work again. "Stop it! Stop it all!" this particular man chanted at the top of his lungs. "There have been no orders to begin!"

But then, two guards, a private and a corporal, came up from behind this particular man; while one held him, the other injected the sedative in his veins.

*Benjamin Harrison,* read the report flashed up on the computer screen.
*Guard*
*47*
*Fifteen years experience*
*Single*
*Fulfilled military commitment*
*Subject to form 5-C and full benefits thereof*

"OK," said the captain, writing something on a piece of paper with a pen.

"Yes, sir?"

"Take this to my secretary," he said to the sergeant, "and then get this Harrison fellow down to the shrinks."

"Retraining, sir?"

"Hopefully," said the captain, taking a cigarette out from the pack on his desk. "Hopefully."

# X

· · · He was a good-sized rat, a rather intelligent rat, and his sleek coat was glossy in the dim light. Man had placed occasional light bulbs where the rat walked, and they lit the horizontal ventilation shaft in a semblance of semi-morning. This rat paused for a moment, his body completely still and at attention, before he started to take a good chew of some plastic insulation that was layered about a copper coaxial cable · · ·

It was reported that for perhaps the first time in the professional career of the Archbishop of Wayne, well, the man slammed a door. Qualification: forcefully slammed a door.

It was rather a fine door. It led to Wayne's office.

Reportedly, Wayne performed that action with not so much grace as strength. The robes of his office rustled as he applied power. His high hat of office quaked with his body as the door, turning on its hinges, compressed the air in its path, then slammed into its frame.

Brother Gates was the observer.

His master was quite irrational, and the subject of Gates's summons was a trivial matter that was not discussed, or so Gates related it to me.

"I have never," the Archbishop reportedly began.

And then without reason Wayne stopped. He flicked his eyes at his assistant, and then stomped the twenty-one feet of carpet to his desk.

"Father?" questioned Gates.

With a grunt the Archbishop, standing before his desk, produced his ring which the monk faithfully kissed. Wayne instantly retracted his hand once the action had been committed, then stormed to the desk chair which he thudded into.

At the desk, Wayne produced a magnifying glass and proceeded to ignore the monk.

"Is something wrong, Father?" Gates asked.

"Brother Gates," Wayne politely replied, with no indication in his voice of what his body was screaming about, "if you wish to refresh yourself while you wait for me, you know where wine resides."

"You are most generous," the monk said.

Gates told me that as he poured himself a burgundy, Wayne produced and pored optically over a rather familiar pocket Bible, his reddish face slowly paling somewhat into a semblance of more normal skin tone.

While Gates was lifting up his wine glass for the first sip, Wayne finished, shoved the book and glass to the top of his desk, and then whispered to all and no one: "Now what meaning does this have?"

"Father?"

There was a knock on the door . . .

. . . The rat spat out the unchewed portions of insulation with a disgusted air. The quality of the product seemed to him to have been going downhill recently. It was getting harder and harder to find top quality, and of course a mate for the rat had recently come of salting age. With a rodent sigh, he decided that now was as good a time as any to wash his handsome face. He did so by spitting into his paws and rubbing vigorously his attractive, finely furred snout and ears. He kept good care of himself, and thought he was a fine catch for a female.

However, the rat was still rather hungry, so he started moving down the basic horizontal shaft, but then suddenly, at an intersection of horizontal shafts, the faint scent of something very attractive could be detected in the rushing air. The rat reared up on his hind legs and took one long, fulfilling sniff, then, like lightning, he scampered down the shaft on the left from whence the scent issued. It had been a long time since the rat had a chance to sink his teeth into a quantity of real, live, actual foodstuff . . .

There was a knock on the door . . .

"Give me a man," Wayne said, letting the pocket Bible return to his fingers. "Give me a man who is not tempted by his pride, or the flesh, or any evil of the mind."

There was a knock on the door . . .

". . . Give me an intelligent man who honestly possesses a shred of humility, dignity—one who believes in the Spirit of God being manifest in the perfection of man, and to that man I shall give my crown and do service to him."

There was a knock on the door.

Gates opened the door slightly and saw the young girl outside with the cross on her forehead.

"Father," he said. "I believe it's your whore."


. . . The rat—his mouth now saliva-filled, for the odor of food was intensifying in his nostrils, his whiskers twitching in the ecstacy of it—hurried down the ventilation shaft, made another correct turn at another intersection, bypassed a blower unit, and all during that time kept his snout high up in the fresh, rushing air. As to where his paws were leading him, the rat had no thoughts of depth on the subject. His brain was engorged only on those shallow ones that led to the eventual filling of his belly . . . and he was very proud of his belly . . .


"You've returned?"

"I'm sorry to have disturbed you at such a late hour."

"How did you know I'd be here?"

"There are no microphones here."

"They did not. . . ?"

"I am a ghost . . . they cannot kill a ghost . . . besides, it was the axman's day off."

"Are you all right, James?"

"I've been with the new King, though I know he's not yet crowned. Away. Away. Oh, he hasn't beat out the competition yet, my dear doctor. My dear woman."

"Competition?"

"His eventual violent death. Away."

"James, you're not well. You shouldn't be. The drugs have probably worn off by now. Come in."

"No. No. It's better that I stay out here and say these few words with you."

"I'm sorry."

I laughed. "I gave my speech before the Archbishop," I said, "as to the perverse nature of his worship, and then as he was sentencing me to my death I was snatched away by death himself."

"James, you're faint."

"Oh, nothing. Nothing. Nothing, Genevieve, my dear! Nothing is— He's made me his right-hand man, now. Death's a catching disease. Minister of Defense. He's tossed so much responsibility on me now, that now . . . it is impossible."

"James."

"Excuse me . . . pardon . . . I . . . it is amazing that I

would now . . . after my brilliant defense that I, my love, over our adultery of Christian thought . . . that now I . . ."

"Shh," she murmured, bending over me. "Oh, my love," she said softly. "Your cheek . . ."

"The hilt of the sword . . . let me get up."

"Stay down for a while."

"I cannot . . . I can't . . . can't you see? I must leave you now . . . there's soon to be a war . . . I must attend a war."

"Oh, James, it's all my fault. You're coming to bed."

"I am a drunkard."

"No, it's the drugs. Can you get up now?"

"Why should I?"

"To get to bed."

"To get to bed . . . to bed . . ."

. . . It was the rat, and only that animal, that came around the corner of the ventilation shaft. In the darkness, his beady black eyes made out what his nose had detected—that which appeared to be food scraps had fallen somehow through a side grate. But the rat was a cautious rat. It was his nose. He halted. And then he sniffed. And the smell of the scraps was almost overpowering, almost demanding to be devoured. Yet in that sniff there was overlaid a hint of ozone. Therefore, the rat turned away. He turned away from a coppery plate that was set before the food—an electronic coppery plate filled with poisonous voltage . . . the rat was bitterly disappointed . . . it was a draw . . . for he was a good-sized rat, a rather intelligent rat, and his sleek coat was glossy in the dim light . . .

# XI

"Ah, there he is," the new King said as I was permitted entry into his informal cabinet room. "See, gentlemen: correctly on time. Punctual. I love punctuality. Perhaps my first royal edict will be to demand that all start on time. For whereas life is brief, and the actions taken within life perhaps important to our physical selves, should not those actions be respected? For if respect is lacking there, we are then disrespectful not only to a second party, but to ourselves."

He tapped his watch with a smile. "Eight hours, precisely," he said.

"Good morning, your highness," I said.

"Good morning, my defense minister. It is indeed a morning worth congratulations. The air's fresh, the sun's warm, the chance of rain is slight."

The three generals exchanged strange looks.

"Tell me, James," the new King said, standing at my side. "Will you breakfast with me?"

"I shall be honored to do so for I hear you have a most excellent cook."

"Yes." The new King laughed. "It is indeed an hour of honor to breakfast and devour his delights, moreso than that of dining with the greatest king."

"How is my lord this morning?"

"Well, James. Well. And I see you've recovered from yesterday's episodes. But enough, we are ignoring these gentlemen here. How goes the war? I hear we have repaired the majority of our surface damages. Is this so?"

"My lord, these gentlemen here would be more expert in such matters. I know for a fact, however, that work has yet to begin on the damaged long system, for the replacement cannon have yet to be manufactured. But this thought, gentlemen. The enemy used a clean weapon. I doubt that the reason for this was a shortage of cobalt sixty or sodium. I fear a darker purpose—invasion. At the moment, the outside radiation level is about twenty Röntgens; it will fall to its normal level of five or six by this weekend. Therefore, the enemy must be one nearby, one that would try to conquer us for control of this area."

The generals perked up their ears at that.

The new King urged me onward.

"We have well substantiated facts," I said, "that there exists an installation similar to ours near the southern shores of Lake Michigan where the city of Chicago used to be. From what our spy satellites have observed, Chicago exists not under a royalty, but under the same type of government which existed in this nation before the war."

"What do you call this government?" General Henderson asked.

"A democracy, though the dictionary's definition of people rule was not the proper definition. We shall not go into corruption. However, according to our intelligence, the only other installation in this state, the Barony of Grand Rapids, was approached by Chicago for an alliance, but the Barony turned it down. However, this was not done out of their alliance with us, but in the name of neutrality."

"Neutrality!" Henderson cried.

"Understand, dear General," I said. "The Barony is barely surviving. What with a population of two thousand, they can barely run their own underground world, much less run an army."

"Yet the Baron did not contact us?" the new King asked.

"No, my lord. I suggest that you contact him. I would wager he declared neutrality to save his country from occupation."

"So be it," said the new King.

"But why would Chicago desire war?" one general whose name I did not know asked. "It makes no sense. The countryside's uninhabitable; will be so except in local patches for the next seventy years. Christ's blood, man, what good's that land?"

"Chicago claims to be the only survivor of the so-called United States of America," I explained. "From what our intelligence can gather, they are completely against any form of royalty. But not churches. In their government, a group of individuals hold the power. They have a legislative body, a judicial body, and an executive who's really only a figurehead to his supporters. No matter—politics shall be discussed later. But figure this: if you had a population of eighteen thousand as has Chicago, and you desired to control the land, what section of it would you want to control?"

"I don't catch your meaning," the new King said.

"The Great Lakes, my lord," I said. "By having military control over the Great Lakes and their outlet, a power would have considerable control over a cheap transportation facility. Plus the fact that Michigan is considerably easier to protect surrounded by water. You cannot stop the air forces, but at least one can get a warning as to an invasion from across the lakes from Tri-Scann."

"What of our arms?" a general cried. "We don't have enough equipment to fight a standing invasion; we've only got nine hundred standing troops now!"

"I am aware of this," I replied. "At eleven hours today, the arms factory, which has been dormant since the founding of the Republic, will be started up to full computer-assisted production. Air Service units have been ordered on patrols already. All reserves are to be called up at six hours tomorrow. In forty-eight hours, we will be at full troop strength—that is, three thousand five hundred men; in ninety-six hours, barring no machinery breakdown, we will have completely gutted ourselves with arms."

"What if they invade before then?" questioned Henderson.

"We have enough equipment to outfit a thousand men," I replied. "Also, we have the Air Service's thirty craft. Hopefully, we will be able to hold them with that."

"What about the economy?" asked another general.

"Is that your worry?"

"No, but . . ."

"Gentlemen," I cut him off. "With the king-successor's permission, there will be a full staff meeting at ten hours this morning to discuss and place in effect our plans. I suggest you and your staffs be present."

They affirmed that they would all be.

"I see," the new King laughed, "that my defense minister has been at work."

"I am starving, your majesty."

"Generals," the new King said. "We must now take our leaves—pardon us. If there are further questions, I am certain James will be able to answer them this morning . . . but we must go to breakfast. Good day."

"I'm certain, gentlemen," I said at the door, "that with your experience and leadership, the Republic will have no worries concerning its defense."

They bade us good day.

"Fools," the new King said in the corridor. "They fell for your reasoning well, James."

"Yes, Robert," I replied. "Who knows, there may be truth

in it. Why a war? It's a question that has been repeated any amount of times. The time is right for Chicago, that's a reason—they must have knowledge of Wayne, and knowledge of the turmoil here."

"It makes no difference, James," the new King said. "Even if there was conspiracy—our hands are tied until one side commits itself. I look at the death of my father, I stop to peer at it, and then my mind weaves plots of ill nature, disease—trivial paps.

"What causes men to become no more than mere celestial chess players?"

"War's a game, my lord."

"That's a trite, lousy explanation of the phenomenon."

"That's because the phenomenon itself is trite."


The King's private dining room was a rather quietly decorated one—twenty by fifty by twenty feet high, with blue walls, and aged oak floors. There was a rectangular walnut table with a pure white tablecloth upon it in the center of the room. A fire burned synthetically in a white marbled fireplace. We entered through what appeared to be a cabinet in the front, but in actuality it was as fake as the hearth flame. A servant stood at a set of double doors that appeared to be the main entrance; there was a smaller door that must have led to the kitchens.

The new King stopped before the fireplace for a moment, peered into the slight warmth-giving illusion, then gave a sort of internalized laugh which resulted in the slight shaking of his shoulders.

He looked up at me with profound silence in his eyes, deep quiet in his face, a stance of nothingness.

"The past will not do," he said.

There were two places set: one at the head of the table, and one at the right of the head.

Without a word, Robert motioned me with his hand to be seated, and I sat on the right. The servant held the King's chair.

"You'd make a good king, James," the new King said as a plate was placed before him.

"Robert?" I said.

"I noticed the manner in which you treated the fools. They felt secure, and we need their security. I think I've made a good choice."

"That's mere speculation, my King."

"Not yet a king," he replied. "I'm still a prince in mourning."

"A king not in name but still one in power."

"I am complimented. Eat."

A simple meal of scrambled eggs and sausages was before us, with coffee and synthetic orange juice. The eggs and sausages were spun soy products, the coffee was natural, and the orange juice—its manufacture was robed in doubt.

"Where were you last evening?"

"I was at a doctor's, Robert. Until five hours this morning."

"So I see," he said, looking at my cheek. "She does good work."

"You must know then," I said cautiously, "that she was the same one who prepared me for trial."

"We know that."

"You had me watched?" I said.

"Tell me one thing," he said, sipping his coffee. "Is she superb in her function?"

I leaned over the table to him as if to whisper. "I'm not certain," I answered softly. "Her cat would not permit me."

"Bah!" The new King laughed.

"Would you like to examine the claw marks on my back?"

"No, no." He laughed on. "I don't believe that will be necessary."

". . . take no excuses. Out of my way! I must see his high-ness!"

"Argument?" the new King said, cocking an eyebrow. With a frown, he beckoned the servant to open the main dining room door.

". . . damned!"

There in the reception room was the Archbishop of Wayne, and as the doors opened he could be seen gesturing violently at another intimidated servant—the servant, a poor young man with brown hair and an expression of absolute terror. He was the one, the only one, who had the bitter choice of receiving either spiritual punishment from his God, or more physical, immediate worldly punishment from his employer. Therefore, it was more than a physical sigh of relief that issued from his lips when he sighted the new King's concern.

"Good morning, Wayne," the King said.

The Archbishop, intent in his tirade against the servant, jumped at the sound of Robert's voice. He bent his body frame and peered in at the occupants of the dining room, his age showing in his face.

"What is the matter, my dear Archbishop? Is your cook ill? Come in! Come in! Do you need breakfast? We could use a blessing."

Slowly the Archbishop turned his head to glare at the servant, but the servant had stiffened back to polite, firm form. Wayne shook his head as if remarking on the quality of help, then straightened up and came forward.

"Good morning, your majesty," he said.

"It may turn out to be," the new King said, digging into his steaming eggs. "But then again, Wayne, all mornings in which one stays alive should be considered 'good.' For is it not 'good' to return from a brief bout with death and be able to speak about it? Enough of this—the philosopher has the best of me today. Would you like some coffee? Food? Come, come, good Father, sit down at my side."

Wayne gave me a stare similar to the one he had granted the intimidated servant; then he took the chair on the new King's left. A setting was placed before him, a cup produced, and coffee, steaming, was poured.

"And how's God today?" the new King asked.

"What?" exclaimed Wayne.

"You are the keeper of His Church, my dear Archbishop. Your arrival here indicates something amiss. Give me a report of it."

"Our Church has been treasoned, your highness," Wayne said.

"Treasoned?" the new King exclaimed politely, folding his hands in attention.

"Perhaps your defense minister there could tell you more about it," Wayne said darkly.

"Treason?" The new King laughed. "James? Would you care to elaborate, Wayne?"

"It was Colonel Sir James Williamson, now defense minister, who claimed our Bible to be a fraud, sir, and now a certain convocation of monks has decided to believe the blasphemy."

"I spoke at my trial backed by history."

"History written by the devil's hand!"

"Gentlemen, gentlemen!" the new King said with a disgusted air. "You will please restrain yourselves."

"Your majesty," I said. "You are well aware of my argument; perhaps there is confusion as to its perspective. I have not charged that Wayne rewrote the Bible, only that his ancestors did, and that Wayne has the ability to restore the true word of God. If this be treason, a statement of fact, then convict and kill me."

"I will not comment on Church law," Wayne replied. "It prohibits criticism of the Church's doctrine leveled by commoners, for they are not in a position to possess a full understanding of it. Your majesty, I do not ask that you charge your defense minister with a crime unless you feel it is necessary. His charges would not change the Church other than bring it back to the level existent before Armageddon. It was his upbringing that led him to it, he being of that time. He can be excused."

"It is rather odd," the new King said with a yawn, "that now after I pulled poor James here from excommunication and death—and believe me I know you intended to have him killed even before you sentenced him—you have the bigness to let him live."

The Archbishop took that silently, then reached into his robes, his silver crucifix dangling, and produced two typewritten sheets of paper which he handed to Robert.

"I found this document on my desk after I finished the morning's High Mass," he said.

"Let's see," the new King said, picking up the document to read. " 'When truth stands corrupt in the public eye . . . when a church exists merely for its own perpetuation and not the spiritual guidance of its members . . .' "

"Lies, of course," the Archbishop muttered. "Total lies."

"Oh, be quiet, Wayne," the King said. "There's more of this to be read. Hmm. Rather poorly written, I might say."

"Unfortunately," Wayne replied, sipping his coffee.

" 'At these times,' " the King continued, " 'it becomes necessary to break free from the bonds of a corrupted institution in order to escape that infection which corrupted it . . . the king, being the product of that institution, may be placed in a position where he may not be able to judge objectively the values of that institution. We ask only that he be fair . . . the thoughts and worships of people are God granted rights, and no man nor institution has the power to infringe upon them . . .' "

"There," said the Archbishop, "the proof of treason lies before your eyes, my lord."

"Who wrote this?"

"His name is there at the bottom."

"Oh, Gates. Conrad Gates. Hmm. I thought he was more original than that."

"He's a traitor to the robe he wears!"

"Quiet, Father, and drink your poison."

Wayne set his coffee back down on the table.

The new King laid the document on the table. "These are

indeed," he said calmly, "words of a serious nature. The thought behind them is of a serious nature, though the words are trite."

The synthetic fire that burned in the electric hearth emitted an artificial crack of burning wood.

Within the kitchen far away down a corridor, someone dropped something metallic on the tile floor.

"Well?" the Archbishop demanded.

"Well, what?" the new King said. "There's your poison, drink it. You do prefer your coffee black? What is truth, my dear Archbishop? Truth is a fiction—so name me a number that isn't a crude scrawling on a piece of paper. Name me a fact—a vapid bare fact, with no clothes allowed. Human beings are beings of abstraction. Truth is a rat devouring wastes, dear Archbishop, truth is the disease he carries, and the sharpness of his bite. No? Truth is felt, not detected. Truth is a cold, bitter life.

"And so we come to sin, as if its determination is filled with much more clarity. What is sin—a lie? I can say that sin is greed, the desire of one for more than what one is worth. Yet who can determine our worth, Father? He can do it, but not on this world.

"In this case, Father, we have no greed. This document asks for nothing, yet it gives something in return. It asks for a voice. So they dare challenge *you*, our future king. What does that matter? Your throne is not secure, eh? Words are fictions, Father, emotions can tell much more than words—words, they are a low form of communication. They claim that a state-supported religion brings about a condition of two self-perpetuating institutions. Is this all truth or lies? They render an opinion, not a judgment. It is subjective human thought, God, and subjective human thought is the stuff reason draws upon, though we dare not admit it. And to repress subjective human thought—God, to possess any desire to destroy another person's thoughts—Wayne, I would claim that as a most total greed."

"For God's sake!" the Archbishop cried, rising from the table.

"You ass," the new King said with a bit of contempt. "Did the poison taste good? Can't you differentiate between the angels of God and the angels of ego? Have you no intelligence?"

"This is condoning trash!"

"What's the matter with trash?" the new King said. "I do not wish rebellion. If the devout are devout, I should doubt that you'd lose attendance. Make martyrs of them, Wayne, and you create secondary Jesuses."

Wayne turned his back to us.

"I think it would be wise," the new King said, "if you donated facilities for Brother Gates. As long as he follows the law laid for the establishment of your Church, I shall have no quarrel with him."

"Donate a chapel!" Wayne screamed, turning about. "You're insane! Your father would—"

"My father is dead!" the new King cried. "I have succeeded to the throne. You will no longer mention my father to me again, do you understand? And you shall obey me."

"This treason is a matter for the Church to decide!"

The King stopped new words with silence.

"Let me make a point clear, Wayne," he said, after a long moment. "If Gates and any member of his movement are being held, they are to be released now. Furthermore, if they are picked up by your monks for any violation, they are to be brought to me."

"You have no jurisdiction!"

"Me, the chosen of God? The blessed bastard? I have an army, Wayne, and if I am forced to take over the duties of your monks— Sir, they will do so!"

The Archbishop backed away ten feet from his chair.

"For these sins," he said quietly, "sir, you will have no confessor. As for the placement of your soul, God will make His decision. As for His Church, you shall be denied of it. Good day, your majesty!"

The Archbishop stalked off.

"Excommunication, Robert?" I said.

A servant brought the new King some wine.

"It was a shallow poison," he said. "Of its name, I do not know. And its effect was subtle—a gradual shrinking of the blood veins unto God, and then, a heart attack. It wasn't the cooks, it was the servants, and they've been replaced and are observed—the food is tested before being placed on the table now. Yes, Wayne is serious about the excommunication."

"But what of your coronation? Who will perform it?"

"Either a new Archbishop, or myself."

"Can he excommunicate a king?"

"He can excommunicate anyone. And I cannot touch him. It would divide the Republic, as would repression."

"Has it ever been done before?"

"My father had the document drafted, but he never signed

it. No, James, a king has yet to be excommunicated." Robert picked up his goblet of wine. "But then," he added, "I always did want to set down some sort of a record in my reign."

# XII

The pilot stood in the Ready Room, his foot on the bench that was implanted in the wall there, and smoked a cigar. He was suited up. It was a small cigar with an ivory tip that he smoked. Plastic ivory tip. Synthetic tobacco. Noncancer forming. A slightly bitter taste to the mouth. They were called commercially, *Pilot Cool-tips*. It was the right sort of thing for a pilot to smoke, particularly this pilot. He didn't give a *damn* about the stupid name. Besides, they were tax-free to him.

The VL-VTO aircraft sat in the flight operations surface compartment. It seated an absolute maximum of four, and it had a port access panel down. A technician was loading some film in the stereovision cameras there. The machine was capable in flight of speeds in excess of thirteen hundred miles per hour. There was a fuel hose stuck into the number two auxiliary tank intake implanted in the stubby starboard wing. Synthetic petroleum product. All synthetic petroleum products were fabricated in the Republic's lab-refineries from the basic raw elements found in their molecular specifications —these raw elements extracted from the Big Fall. The fuel was called, noncommercially, *Grade #3H*. It was, of course, the *right* kind of fuel for this type of VL-VTO craft, serial number R12-56.

The pilot was staring at his helmet on the bench when the order came to commence operations through the Ready Room intercom. Silently, efficiently, he ditched the cigar on the dirty floor and ground it out with his right foot.

Destroying the flame of the cigar had given the pilot's right foot something to do other than brace the pilot's body against the bench. The pilot grabbed his helmet, spread the edges of it, put it on, and sealed it on the titanium suit ring that ran about his suit's collar. The faceplate was up. The pilot opened the gun metal gray painted metal door, and briskly walked into the flight operations surface compartment.

The technician stood back from the opened port access panel, and pressed a button on a control which he held in his

100

right palm. With a sigh, the panel folded back into its molded place. The technician looked up at the pilot, who was standing by the nose of the aircraft. A hatch was there, with a titanium ladder leading up to the green lighted cockpit. The compartment's floodlights played over the pilot's helmet—his face was dark with shadow. The faceplate gleamed in the light. The pilot looked at the technician, who was staring at him, started to say something, but controlled the urge. He put his right hand on the ladder, then suddenly turned and looked back at the door to the Ready Room. For a moment he stared at it, then he turned back and looked up into the cockpit. Small, green . . .

". . . look tired, James."

"Perhaps. Perhaps. Am I late?"

"No, you're on time, love."

"Excellent. Most excellent. May I sit next to you?"

"But of course you . . ."

. . . lights led the way. In a series of fluid, precise motions, he stepped up the ladder, and climbed up and into the command seat.

As he fastened the safety harness, the pilot looked down between his legs and watched the titanium ladder fold itself up. As he plugged in his life-support hoses, he saw the technician peer up at him with a silent face through the still-open hatch. The pilot wanted to make some sign, some indication of recognition, but he controlled himself. The technician seemed to be staring at something next to the pilot . . .

"Aren't all these people exciting, Sir James? Have you ever just sat down on a bench some time and watched your fellow man pass by? See these men? My, that brown-haired one—isn't he handsome? Maybe he's a millionaire, or a man bound to make a million, and he's telling his friends . . . and he's telling his friends . . ."

"What is he telling his friends?"

"That woman there—she, the one with age. She's pretty with silver hair, does it up nice, don't you think? She had a body men went after and she's kept it up. Wears the modern fashions to keep up the flow of diminished competition. And now she's shopping—tracking down the bargains, and looking for a man, any man . . . for she's old now, not young now, Sir James, and she wants someone to help her live her old age gracefully, James, peacefully."

"She has to wait."

"We all have to wait, Sir James. We are . . ."

. . . but it wasn't anything important, for the technician moved back, and the hatch drew itself shut and was sealed.

The pilot reached into his suit's right shoulder and withdrew a brown paper envelope with a *Secret* classification stamp on it. He tore it open, and removed a piece of film from it, which he placed in a wrist holder that was strapped on the outside of his suit. During this time his eyes were fixed on the computer-run status check that played on the control board monitor. With the film in place, he removed a recording cassette from the envelope and plugged it into a slot on his left. A map, its code information, replaced the status check on the monitor. The windshield was a bit dirty. He pressed a button and flipped a switch on and sat quietly for a while, then reversed the procedure. The wiper arms reburied themselves in the nose. The pilot glanced at his watch. He plugged in his radio, and signaled that he was ready. The command to start engines was given. The pilot flipped the proper switches, and carefully watched the jump of the needles within their gauges. A horn was blown outside the craft. The ceiling rolled back and let the sun in. He experienced a slight nervous tremor as the deck of the flight operations surface compartment was raised up to the top of the surface mound. The command to commit was given. The pilot grabbed the control stick, revved up his engines, hit the gravity button, and then the craft gracefully lifted up and headed . . .

"The prince is to be excommunicated."

"James, you're kidding!"

"What did you expect? A certain group of monks led by Brother Conrad Gates broke free of the Church; his highness refused to put down the rebellion. For God's sake, woman, did you think Wayne's that much a man?"

"What are you going to do, James?"

"What is there to do? Huh? Watch my activities, my life —dark corridors. I'm rather amazed that you didn't ask about the pistol I'm carrying."

"You're not a killer, James."

"One night of understanding, huh? I have killed many people."

"You're a soldier."

"The result is still the same."

The conductor bowed slightly to the luncheon applause, then turned to his stand where the music was laid open for his eye's inspection. As for tradition, he left the baton on the podium, and with a flick of his wrist directed the orchestra to play. No trumpets or horns or drums. Mozart. *Symphony No. 40 in G minor, K550*. The audience of five hundred, trapped within this sound, sight, and orchestral feel, quietly ordered lunch in whispers from soft-spoken waiters. The conductor was slow. The orchestra dragged. The woodwinds were dull.

. . . southwest. The sky was clear. As the VL-VTO gained altitude in the clear, clean sky, the radiation level began to fluctuate. At twenty thousand feet it was thirty-one Röntgens compared with the ground's eighteen. At forty-five thousand feet it dropped to five. The pilot steered clear of clouds, for he knew the fallout dust would be trapped within them.

At sixty thousand cloudless feet, the pilot leveled off his climb, and picked up speed to about six hundred miles per hour. His stereovision cameras cut on. He extended a long, wire-like antenna from the aircraft's tail for better transmission. The fuel gulped down the fuel lines—the engines were hungry, even if they were assisted by the gravitation field units. The VL-VTO soon crossed the outer edges of the desert, to the lands where life existed and had been tampered not by such things as water, sand, and wind erosion. The ruins of Detroit were soon far behind him. He armed the light M/C cannon jammed into the nose of his craft, and checked his rocketry. He could very well expect visitors. He could very well expect anything at . . .

"What does this all mean to me?"

"Simply, Genevieve, this: Don't ever see me again."

"But I . . ."

"They will be watching you. I can only add to your penalty. They will find some excuse in which to close in and do some harm."

"Oh, look at the people here!" she exclaimed.

"Listen to me! Speak to me!"

"See that boy with the group over there, Sir James? Now, he's a student who's going to be . . ."

"It's for our good, can't you understand that?"

"I can understand," she said, with her eyes in flames. "If we were to go our separate ways, Sir James, what would be our good then? What value would it have?"

"No value," I said.

. . . all. Below him, a group of buzzards were orbiting, ten miles from the desert area now, orbiting probably over a dead animal. The pilot didn't care. The pillaged remains of a small town, untouched by the devastation of both recent and old bombs, passed by. Radiation levels dropped, formed pockets, did not exist in some areas. There were surface pockets still fit for human occupation. Not many humans. A family or two now inbred so deeply that reproduction was not desirable. Clouds began to pick up below the pilot, and to his side. Soon, he was one hundred straight miles from the Republic, turning straight toward Chicago, dropping altitude. A radar/Tri-Scann warning light went on. The pilot looked up instinctively. There was a jet above him. There were three jets above him.

With his left hand, the pilot shoved off the safety mechanisms on his weaponry, and started to track his targets. He had been detected. This far north. The aircraft, fixed wing variety, peeled off toward him. The pilot flipped the ECOM switch, and in a five-second burst the notice of his detection, position, altitude, number of aircraft, type, and course, was flashed back to base.

As the jets closed in, in formation, the pilot jammed his throttle forward, dived to a level five thousand feet lower than where he had been, executed a turn, saw the solution light on his computer monitor, and fired two air-to-air missiles. They lashed out in a twin series of white foamy streaks, their rocket flames hidden in their thrusts.

The required signal came in on his radio from his superior officers. The pilot ejected the camera pod, spun and swerved again on his enemy in time to see a missile miss one plane and its brother trace and tear apart another.

The jets had Chicago markings on them.

One aircraft zipped by, firing a stream of M/C fire, missing.

There was a missile from the other.

The pilot instantly brought the VL-VTO down, watching the altimeter fall and the speed rise. The missile circled and dived after him. He passed the sound barrier as he passed the twenty-thousand-foot level. The gravitation field started to dig in on the effects of acceleration. The automatics tried to pull the VL-VTO aircraft out of the dive. The pilot overrode them. The missile was closing. The ground, all greenish and brown, with bits of blue and tan and gray, came spinning upward. The pilot watched the altimeter. At five thousand feet he started to pull up, jerking the throttle into its most forward position. The frame of the aircraft screamed. Pressures shot up. The craft began to ascend when it reached the nine-hundred-foot level. Its air speed was close to two and one half times the speed of sound. The pilot, even with gravity assistance, was near blacking out. The missile slammed into the earth, producing a fireball one hundred and ten feet in height.

The two remaining Chicago jets were waiting for him at ten thousand feet.

The pilot watched them scatter, one to the left and one to the right. He dived after the one that went to the left. The pilot took a tighter turn than his enemy. A slightly higher centrifugal force pressed the pilot into the bottommost part of his seat. The enemy, perhaps a little less capable, perhaps a little careless, came into the pilot's sights. The pilot triggered his M/C cannon. Fire, tiny little bursts of flame, appeared on the Chicago jet, but then . . .

"James," she said quietly. "They'll be after me too for my connections to Gates. I'm a minister in his Church. You and I both know what a farce Wayne's Church is. The affectation . . . James, I'm a Christian, but I'm a woman too, and as a woman . . . the depth of my feeling . . ."

. . . the other jet appeared on the VL-VTO's tail. The pilot hit the throttle, pulled up, and attempted a loop. His short barrage at the Chicago jet had taken its total account. The silent streams of anti-photons first had caused smoke to appear from the craft, then real flame, and then ejection of that craft's pilot to a death more slow, perhaps more horrible, than that of being slammed into the earth.

The pilot looked down from the underside portion of his loop, looked down by craning his neck upward, and saw the remaining craft turning out of his way. He pulled up from his loop in a spin, righting himself, and let the Chicago jet come up to meet him. Twisting away from the enemy's fire, the pilot turned about to get the jet in his sights, but his opponent executed a series of maneuvers that caused the pilot to dive to get out of the way. In the process, the VL-VTO took some shots in the starboard wing, shuddering in the force of them. The pilot instantly hit a starboard placed control that caused a foam to mix with the fuel in the tank there, resulting in a camouflaging smoke. His opponent was an intelligent man who came in for the kill. The pilot dodged, throttled back, and his attacker streaked past him. The pilot got him in his sights, fired. Slight damage . . .

"Look at that woman there," I said. "She's dressed well. Perhaps it's only for work, you know, or maybe it's for her husband or her husband-to-be, or maybe that man who finally decided to give her a try. Her cheeks are almost red in expectation of it, and notice how her body moves."

"James," she said.

"Perhaps," I replied softly, "as minister of defense and confidant to our new King, I can be manipulated just as easily as I was for my failed martyrdom."

"Well," she said, "if you believe that . . ."

"I believe in nothing," I said. "At times, I even doubt that misplaced faith, that dream-pledge that I committed upward to a faceless deity some call 'God.' It's funny. I used to believe in life as a youth, then death; both have disappointed me . . . I mean, now. . . look around you. You can see the faces and bodies in motion—the shells of reality. At times I wake up and see the animal in man, and at those times I'm frightened, for it takes only a moment for me to realize that I'm a member of that race too. And when you take a man, love, and you peel his skin away from him and peer into his inner depths . . . well, we all haven't a shred of light inside of us—the cavity's as black as Hell. We are diseased inside, all of us. We are filled with rot. In some, the infection has taken a bad turn for the worse; in others, the infection has yet to reach the highest stage of development. But that stage will come.

"You call this living, love? Let's call it what it is—a long obituary, nothing more. Even in my time, it was quite the same. A government totally out of touch with its people and more concerned with itself than the world. And there was war in the background, always war. If my country did not supply the arms, the rival country did. For some odd reason —perhaps because they possessed a foundation which, idealistically at least, had some basis of humanity—the religions practiced by man were the only institutions concerned with the semblance of truth. They called for brotherhood, but the living were arranging their burials. We were too busy for love. Many 'Christians' worshiped out of fear, from the past, the present, possibly the future. Fear was respectable. It still is. And there were religious leaders, oh, great ones, who strutted out on stage with sickening pride, playing up to that respectable fear for the satisfaction of their egotism, and their greed. Yes, fear, as we all know, is perhaps a better tool for domination than any human infection."

"You don't believe in me?"

"I may," I said. "In time."

"James," she said, sighing. "Sir James—are you going to leave me?"

"For what? To maintain my honor? I have none at the moment. Pride, yes, that I have—those in rebellion are sick with it. Redemption from past sin? Not even the Church as it exists now could twist what we have done together into a web of it. Genevieve, people are going to die."

"Soon?"

"I fear it will be soon."

"And us?"

"And us . . . and us . . ."

The enemy pitched down in a shallow dive with the pilot hot on his tail. The Chicago jet came into the pilot's sight once more. It was only for a few seconds. The pilot fired. Again, only slight damage.

The pilot shot past the enemy before he had a chance to avoid it, then on second choice banked to the east and looped upward unexpectedly, causing the opponent's salvo to miss by a good fifty feet. But as the pilot maneuvered into position to jump at the jet once more, the Chicago pilot had outdone his efforts, and the VL-VTO took a battery amidships. The cabin was laced open at the back. The suit clamped on, tight. It began to be difficult to maintain trim. The Chicago jet closed in. The pilot pitched left. The jet followed. The pilot dived his VL-VTO downward with the enemy's shots just missing his tail.

Without thought, the pilot jammed full throttle and brought the nose of his ship up. Acceleration forces pinned the pilot back. His blood pounded in his veins by the force of it; his heart tried to counteract the forces that were now attempting to drive his fluids downward to his stomach. The Chicago jet, caught by surprise, was slow in answering. It rushed broadside across the pilot's sights. The M/C cannon fired. Striking amidships, and moving back, the entire back of the Chicago jet broke open. Its fuel exploded. The jet separated into four parts and a massive fireball. The clear, clear sky was streaked in black, oily smoke. The pilot began to circle around the smoke to see if his opponent had somehow made it clear.

There was . . .

"We are," I said, "to lead secret lives apart. Let no one know of us until the violence has gone away. My body may endanger yours. I cannot permit it."

"And what if I am to die?" she said.

"It's the time," I said. "It's the quality of the time that runs against us."

"James."

"Good day, Doctor . . . I . . . Good day."


. . . a sigh as a catch was released on the hatch while the remains of the decontamination shower was still beading up on the polished skin of the VL-VTO, and flooding the jagged tears of metal where M/C cannon fire had found its mark. The ladder lowered automatically. The technician stared up at the pilot in the cockpit seat. The pilot was surrounded by flight control lights that tinged his helmeted face slightly green.

The pilot stared down for a moment, then slowly began to remove his helmet.

The technician's white, clean face was emotionless. The technician's face was plain, devoid of any remarkable feature save a mouth that didn't appear to be there.

The pilot unstrapped himself, then carefully removed the film from his wrist holder and stared at it for a long time.

The technician stepped far back as the pilot climbed down the ladder, dropped his flight log recordings in a large lead case that was waiting by the ladder, and stopped to look up at his craft. The right landing gear had never deployed for the landing; the left gear and the nose gear left the craft tipped in a bizarre way to the right. Slowly, the pilot stepped off toward another door implanted in the wall of the flight operations surface compartment.

At that door, the pilot stared at the Ready Room door for another long moment, then twisted the handle, and entered a long passageway that led elsewhere.

For, in the immediate future, the pilot planned to be ill for a few days; but he was certain that the chances of his recovery were good.

# PART 3

# Variations

# XIII

It was one of the night servants, a male about forty years old, his bald skull gleaming in the hallway's lights, who gave an imploring look and said: "Your majesty."

Perhaps the new King didn't want his assistance.

It was difficult for anyone to determine what the new King desired.

"Silence!" he bellowed, dressed in his sleeping clothes and his robe, with his hair spun and twisted about by naked sleep, and a half-aware look in his eyes. "Everybody!" he rasped out in a voice that seemed to be stuck somewhere in its gearing. "Silence!"

The cleaning maids looked up from their knees from down the hall.

A robot floor-sweeper-polisher stopped in its tracks.

A man who was making a slight adjustment in the alignment of an oil painting on the wall dropped his hands to his sides as if he were a thief being caught.

There was a dirty, soapy-water smell in the air.

A vacuum machine in a nearby room electronically clicked and sighed; its sounds vanished in a sea of lessening wheezes and groans.

"Give me silence!" the new King roared, his voice still tinged with the gravel of his unconsciousness, his back bending, his palms hard into his ears.

"Call for the royal physician," the bald servant told a

curious boy who had come up from the kitchens. "And *walk* to get him—softly, now."

"This noise," the new King was heard to say. "This horrible, terrible noise. What is making all this noise? It sounds like stomping, the blocks of concrete slamming together, or a factory at peak work. And that rushing sound —like the breath of some monster, panting and panting. My dear God. God. Oh my God. William, we haven't been breached, have we?"

The servant caught the new King in his arms, righted him, then told him that all was normal with the world.

"No," the new King said, backing away down the hallway. "There is nothing normal with this world tonight. The moon tonight is ringed with orange cloud. The sun will be covered by gray, darkish cloud, and fires shall be brilliant with flame. And if on the morrow's night the moon's been stolen away . . . then . . . then . . ."

"The moon, your highness?" the servant said.

"But then,". the new King went on as if he hadn't paused, "this noise." He gave his body a slight twist downward, to the right, as if struck by pain. "All is not well," he said. "My dear Lord, all has never been well."

"My lord!"

"Look, he falls!"

"The doctor—quick!"

"My, my," a maid said down the hallway, dropping her scrub brush into a hot bucket. She was an older woman, nearly fifty years old. "The King's fainted." She shook her head.

She then reached into the pocket of her apron and took out a plastic hand control. "Come on, baby—there's a dear," she cooed as a robot emerged from the wall. "Clean up this floor for Granny."

"Who comes?"

"Do not shoot me, friend."

"Issac?"

"Who would you expect at such an hour?"

"Come up and be recognized!"

"Go to bed!"

"That's my intention."

The fresh guard paused at the top of the stairs, turned himself awkwardly about, scanning the skies, then walked up on the platform, clasping the shoulder of the guard who sat in the gunnery chair facing the desert plain to the south.

The dome was very new and very clean.

"How goes it tonight, Herbert?"

"I got one lined up for me."

"Free?"

"What do you think?"

"Oh," the fresh guard said, laughing, running his gloved hand over the bottom of his helmet in an unconscious manner as if to rub a beard there. "I think the other."

"You think wrong then, friend."

"You always have to pay in the end, anyway," the fresh guard said, "no matter how you take it at first, friend. Dammit, it's horribly hot in these suits—the standards are better. It's inhuman to subject loyal soldiers to the demands of this equipment."

"This equipment, friend, will insure your children the opportunity to feel light."

"Light? Smight! A man can't go around being weighed down like this. And what if nature calls? A flood, that's what! Maybe worse!"

"It's good for you." Herbert laughed. "Builds up those old muscles."

*"Bah!"* Issac said with a disgusted shake of his hand. "Well, anything odd or unusual to report?"

Herbert picked up a clipboard that he had been resting on his knee, then looked at some recently installed instrumentation before him. "Nope," he said. "Some slight local radiation ground glows—they're up on the chart and in the computer too. Background radiation showing the expected decline. I don't know why in hell they got us taking readings up here; they all get the same information from the stuff in Defense Command."

"Confirmation," Issac said, pressing a check-in code on the computer station in the observation dome. "OK. Take it easy, Herbert," he said as the man got off the gunnery chair and tried to stretch. Issac took over the chair. "Don't work too hard in your sleep, now."

"I'll take it nice and easy," Herbert said, smiling as he reached the top of the stairs. "Oh, and hey! About those local ground glows. There's one real close to us, probably about a mile away at oh-two-one-oh degrees, one minute flat."

Issac turned to that direction and leaned in toward the glassite. "Dim the lights a bit more," he said.

Herbert did so.

"Humph!" Issac said, looking at the glow. "That doesn't look like a radiation glow to me—too damn bright. Bluish. No, maybe it's dim enough. I don't know. If it starts winking at me, or sending Morse, I'll have utter demons drag you out of bed, no matter how disappointed the pretty lady will be."

Herbert turned back and began to walk down the stairs. "So this is what I get for being responsible?" he said.

. . . eyes flashing, the kangaroo rat paused at the entrance of his burrow, his handlike paws clutched in a sort of prayer—his nose quivering and alive. The moon could shine off his whiskers. His fur was sleek and would be clean in that shine. His pert, active ears were upraised and soft; like blackened white diamonds the kangaroo rat's eyes gleamed in it all.

The air was somewhat fresher this evening than that of the recent past.

The rat inhaled and exhaled the air in quick breaths, but this kangaroo rat was a particular kind of rat, and in his own special way he savored the atmosphere.

To the south of the rat's burrow there were the surface floodlights of the Republic, and the newly reconstructed observation bubbles—the entire mess a series of metallic, concrete, and radiation glass blotches on the torn-up ground, or so the rat thought.

This kangaroo rat was an intelligent, realistic rat who knew where he stood in the world, and although he did not understand the world, he was secure within his innocence.

On a small billow of luminous smoke, with some slight sparks of errant flame, a VL-VTO craft took off from the concrete surface mound, paused for a moment at an altitude of about twenty feet, then streaked off to the southwest.

The kangaroo rat, being by all means of simple mind and humble means, shallowly shrugged his shoulders. He didn't have too much of an understanding of the Republic, for he could only see what went on, on the surface, and that was something rather confusing to him. He realized that he was not in a position to judge whether or not there was any depth to the matter. Certainly, at times in the past, the rat had wondered about the strange metallic beings that came out of the concrete surface mound doors and walked about. They had two arms, walked upright, and spent their time either messing around with other metallic and strange-shaped objects, or built weird things on the ground, or worked around pits that closed themselves up. They also drove vehicles about. And vehicles drove themselves about. Who drove what the rat was not certain. Being, as stated before, an intelligent rat, the kangaroo rat had theorized that these strange metallic creatures could possibly be related to ants, for in the kangaroo rat's rare day travels he had observed the ant at work. Yet this theory gave no satisfaction to the kangaroo rat, for the strange metallic creatures had only four arms to the ants' six, and were rather gigantic in size in relationship to their cousins—therefore, they should have had eight or ten or twelve, or some such number.

As to the outcome of this theory, as to everything, the rat had but one solution. He shallowly shrugged his shoulders.

With a spring from the entrance of his burrow, the rat was off into the night.

Being a peaceful rat, this kangaroo rat lived off what little vegetation he could gather during the cloudless, rather cold night. He didn't have too much competition. His mate had passed away a few weeks ago, and there had been no litter.

Brooding on this, the rat stopped to nibble on some small blades of grass that had somehow struggled to live in the bad soil.

He had loved his mate very dearly, and she had loved him. They had chanced to meet one night, and being lonely, they had soon adopted each other. But she had taken ill, and there was nothing he could do about it.

But then the ground started to tilt up.

The rat stopped all that he was doing, shivered for a second, then got rather mad, for he didn't know what the hell was going on.

Slowly, with a grinding sound, the soil that the rat's feet rested upon began to rise up toward the clear stars, and it all seemed rather a permanent change.

However, the kangaroo rat was mad, very mad, for once before this had happened to him, and he'd be damned if he was going to pick himself up again from the eventual scrap heap at the bottom. Therefore, with much courage—well, call it pluck—the rat dug in with his powerful legs, and hopped up the incline, barely making it to the top as the soil beneath him started to give way.

Up to the top, and away.

Was it the rat's fault that once he had cleared the top there was no place else to go but thirty feet down, into the rising maws of some air quality analysis equipment?

"Good evening," I called from the bottom of the stair.

"It's morning," Issac said, a jigger annoyed. Then he gave forth the standard greeting: "Who comes here?"

"Sir James Williamson."

"Rank?"

"Defense Minister."

There was a moment's silence. "You don't expect me to believe that one, do you?" Issac said.

"Yes, or I'll have your stripes."

"I don't have any. Are you in the regulation equipment for the day?"

"Yes."

"Advance then with identification displayed, and be recognized."

"By God, sir, I'm sorry," Issac said as he looked me over at the top of the stair.

"My compliments," I replied, putting my identification card back into one of the outer breast pockets of my radiation suit.

We looked like two monsters together; the visors retracted so that our bare heads stuck out of the massive suits, our bodies rather sluggish under the forty-pound weight.

The guard awkwardly replaced his laser pistol in his holster.

"How goes the evening?"

"The morning goes well, sir," the guard replied neutrally, turning to the instrument panel where several dials glowed like animals' eyes.

"It's morning already?"

"Exactly two hours and thirty-one minutes, sir, into the day."

"I'll be damned."

"So we are, sir."

I scanned the surrounding surface outside the dome which appeared to me in a surreal way due to the effects of the floodlights. Farther out from the beams, spottily placed in the depressions of the earth, were strange glows of a sort I had not witnessed before.

"Tell me, Issac," I said. "What are those, out there beyond the parameter?"

"Those, sir?"

"Those . . . strange lights."

"Radiation glow."

"Caused by what?"

"Inequal distribution of the fallout from that recent attack."

"Stay away from those, eh?"

"Yes, sir."


. . . trapped in the mind, the mind, the mind, the mind, he thought as he stared up from the cool comfortable table and watched the soft metal probes being lowered toward his skull. Gone, far gone, forever away, he thought. Disease, rot, and decay lift off the bone, and the brain's all mush inside— gray stinking mush fit for the Big Fall. The Big Fall.

The nurse, her uniform particularly taut over her breasts, her body covered with perfume, held this particular man's hand as the delicious contact was made.

. . . bending over the panel, the doctor watched neutrally as needles fluctuated. Activity. An oscilloscope danced a photonic line across its greenish window of the mind. A shiver ran through the body of this particular man as an ECG was taken which showed his heart still alive, still in control.

. . . no, no, no, the entire component is damaged, he thought. The transistors, all of them are blown. The complex printed sub-sub-miniature circuitry—all burned out and shorted. Oh, smell that smoke. The transformers no longer perform. All the insulation's gone.

Cleaning out the synapses, boy.

Cleaning out the synapses and restoring the old dendrites to their former outstretched glory.

Run the personality profile tapes.

. . . the mind, the mind, the mind, he thought.


Staring at the texture . . .

. . . stoppp

. . . of the soils . . .

. . . stoppp

. . . that about the observation dome . . .

. . . stoppp

. . . were laid.


I looked up and found the guard, Issac, sitting back in the gunnery chair, in the shadow of the deactivated M/C cannon, his face hidden in the cavern of his open helmet.

"Tell me, Issac," I said. "How goes your world?"

"It goes fair to well, sir."

"Fair to well?"

"Fair in that we are permitted life in it, sir—well in that the opportunity of a tomorrow will come to be."

"They say the new King is mad."

"Aye, sir—they do, although I wonder about those voices."

"Why, because of the robes they wear?"

"Aye." Issac laughed. "And the crucifixes they wear around their pretty necks."

"I take it, then, you're perhaps one who is full of the latest gossip?"

"We call it crap, sir."

I smiled at that.

"What do you think of the rebellion in the Church, then?"

"What's there to think, sir?" Issac replied. "That new bishop—what's his name, Gates is it? Gates it is. So he claims that Wayne's Church violated the New Testament by 'rewriting it,' and therefore produces some copies that look like they came from before the Great War. Big Deal. For one, Gates could have faked the books, and some do say they're poorly written. So could have Wayne; what are we arguing about? The point is this—what does it matter? Just another bunch of egotists arguing that there is such a thing as a divinity—if that was so, you and me, sir, we wouldn't be here spouting off."

"You don't believe in God."

"I believe, yes. I believe in the divinity of man, for I think mad men created God, not the other way around. So what if we're the end product, as some say, of an ocean of boiling proteins? Does that really matter?"

"What about Christ?"

"He may have existed," the guard said, looking off into the night. "I can believe in that. But he was just a man, nothing more than you or me, no superman. Perhaps he was the perfect man."

"Then why do you attend a Church at all?"

"For that question, sir," Issac replied, "there are three answers. One: I would lose my position. Two: If I did not attend, well, the penalty is excommunication. Three: Even with that penalty, the Church tries to preach that we should love our fellow man. That hypocrisy is so entertaining, the price is well paid."

We became silent. I lightly touched the railing on which my arm rested with a gloved hand, feeling almost nothing.

There was a flash of something outside, and a darkening. A cloud system was moving swiftly in.

An alarm sounded.

It sounded like a horn fracturing in mid-note.

"What the hell?" Issac cried, jumping out of his seat.

Then he was at the instrumentation panel, slapping a few toggle switches down. A computer screen lit up. Several dials swung into action. The lights in the dome went off.

Upon the screen a Tri-Scann ground image was projected, a series of fluctuating yet distinct electronic images.

"Boogies," Issac said into his helmet mike mechanically. "Eleven of them. Ground speed three miles per hour. Bearing now two hundred and twenty degrees flat. Arrival time approximately ten minutes. Range about five hundred and twenty-eight yards."

As he was saying this, a light flashed on the control panel readout.

## CONDITION YELLOW

Issac pressed a number combination on a digital bank of push button switches, and a screen next to that displaying the electronic blobs lit up yellowishly. There were several red—brilliant red human forms on it.

The computer started to think—I could feel it thinking— and conclusions began to be read off.

"What do you think?" I asked.

Issac looked up from his work. "Surface people," he said neutrally. "Probably unarmed."

"Dear God, what do they want from us here?"

"I don't know," Issac said. "It . . . could . . .

" . . . for it's work, work, work, in the factory . . ."

" . . . be . . .

" . . . for the money spent on booze . . . "

" . . . almost . . .

" . . . and don't forget the darling lass . . ."

" . . . anything."

" . . . from the agency you choose . . ."

"Who comes?" said Issac, his voice a reflex.

"W-what?"

"Who comes?"

There came the voice of a guard who should have been posted elsewhere: "It's his majesty."

"Are you in today's equipment?" Issac asked.

There was silence for a moment.

"He is," the other guard answered. "I helped him with it myself."

"Advance then," Issac said. "And welcome, your majesty."

Legs started to mount the concrete stairway. I walked over to the top of it. "Good evening, your majesty," I said.

"James?" he said, looking up. "That's funny. That's really funny. Oh, it's morning, James, and I'm drunk in it all."

I gave him a hand to help him up the final two steps. "So I see, your majesty," I said.

(" . . . infrared readings completed. Standby preliminary RAD/scann," Issac murmured to himself.)

"Is it a cold night, James?" the new King asked.

"That depends on one's perceptions," I said.

"And therefore," he replied, "it depends on one's mind."

"They will soon be in sight."

"They?" the new King said softly, turning about.

"My lord," I said, "we've picked up on our screens what appears to be a party of people heading our way."

"People?" the new King blurted, his voice rising. His head instantly turned to scan the hidden horizon. "Where? Are they armed?"

"Not from our data, your majesty," Issac said. "We count about eleven on foot, with little metallic content."

"Where?" the new King commanded, striding up to the railing and pounding his hands down on it.

"There, your majesty," Issac said, pointing. "About a hundred yards off, now."

"Light," the King said. "Give me light on them. I want to see them."

"The spotlights will pick them up pretty soon," I said.

A shiver seemed to run through the new King's frame.

It was a shiver so intense that I could feel it through the radiation suit.

"How can anyone live out in that mess we have created? It's no good for men," the new King said. "We left it that way. How can they survive?"

"They're probably barbarians," Issac said quietly. "They probably live in the ruins to the south, where it just might be possible, my lord, for some sort of a life."

"My God. God. It can't be dreams this night."

"There!" I cried. "Over there!"

"My dear sweet Jesus!" the new King cried.

It was a group of four men, three women, and four children of various ages. They were almost naked. The light and the night's shadow played over their lack of clothing, picking up the patches of dirt on their bodies, and other things not as pleasant or natural. They wore about themselves, from what could be seen, various faded rags and some animal skins. Two of the men carried their young, a boy for one man and a girl for the other. There was a man leading the way with his assistant close behind him, and then the two men with their burdens, the women, and the remaining children. One of the women was limping badly. One of the children was walking as if he had no stomach and had to use his hands to hold his guts in.

They were walking toward us now.

"We're in such a gray world," the new King said, slumping to the floor.

"My lord?"

"We're too evil, James, to be in the light, and too damned religious to be in the interior of utter Hell."

"Are you all right, your majesty?"

"Oh, James, just let me sit for a while."

"Are you certain you're not ill?"

"I'm as fit as a bastard should be. It's the drink. Only the drink."

"They're up to us, sir!" cried Issac.

I turned. The floodlights were now displaying their more obvious features.

"Holy—" I said. "Get the emergency medic team ready by the archway. Standard contingency on my commencement orders. Who's got the watch tonight in Defense Command?"

"Timpkins, sir," Issac said. "You can plug in there."

"All right, thanks, now move!"

They stopped about twenty feet in front of the observation dome. They stood. They did not sit. They made no detectable noise; they were silent. They seemed to be staring intently into the dome as if they could make out we three men who were inside of it, beneath the harsh green exterior glare.

Burned, they were.

They were burned with skin that was browned or blackened, flaking-off, or soon to be flaking-off, skin; distorted human faces. They were either bald, or soon to be. The women's bodies were all swollen and reddish in hue. The children were silent and still. The leader had a patch over his right eye—that side of his face had been charred.

Shreds of something hung down from the arm of the assistant leader—it appeared to be skin mixed with an attempted cloth bandage.

"Brothers." The new King moaned to the floor. "Oh, where are they? My brothers in butchery?"

"They're dead," I said. "This is our final product, do you see? Torn of their dignity, they have come instinctively to us for our help, though we can do little but ease the tremendous pain of transition for them. Full of strontium, cobalt, and the rest. Their bodies are tearing themselves apart before our very eyes.

"And for what? The perpetuation of a dream? A childish image of masculinity?"

"Horrible," the new King muttered softly to the floor. "Horrible, horrible, horrible . . ."

"It's amazing that they could make it here at all," Issac said.

"Horrible . . ."

"Is the team ready yet?"

"They'll soon be. They're getting their equipment on now."

"Horrible . . ."

"We are the ones with guilty stamped on our foreheads."

"My God!" the new King screamed. "My God!"

"My lord?"

I turned to see the King rise.

"They're around, James! They're around us! Us! They're all over us! Murderers. Murderers! They're going to kill us, oh dear Jesus. *My brain's on fire!*"

"Robert!"

I grabbed him.

He did not struggle, but twisted about in a sort of fit, of anguish, of terror, pain, and ecstacy of cruelties.

But in a moment that was over, the sweat began to pour down the new King's brow; he was cold and calm once more, and without a word he removed my hold on him.

"Are you all right, my lord?"

"It's over," he said quietly, walking toward the stair. "It's all over."

"My lord?"

He stopped at the stair's top.

"Kill them," he said.

"Who?"

"I need not specify. Use the anti-personnel laser so that they don't feel the pain."

"That's murder, my lord!"

"I am King, James."

"Robert!"

"Obey me, James."

And then, without another word, the new King turned and started down the stairs.

"For God's pity, my lord!"

He was silent.

"For the love of God!"

He continued down into the Republic.

"Coward!"

He disappeared from my sight.

"Goddamned coward!"

The cannons were lined up for the execution.

The spotlights focused directly on the group so that accuracy could be assured.

Issac looked up from the control panel, ready to give the final word through me to Defense Command.

"What are they doing now, sir?" he asked.

I looked away from a star I knew far-off and away from here, and looked at the group.

"They're praying," I said.

# XIV

There was just one candle placed on the marble-like altar, bearing a thin flame, a slender candle made of wax with a black wick. The Archbishop of Wayne muttered words in dead languages over it, his breath making the flame waver in ecstacy from its force.

Before the stereovision cameras, the new King held out a crown, a gold-colored one his father had worn on formal occasions, with a cushioned, black velvet lined interior that had been fitted by hand to match the new King's skull.

I jerked the door violently open. The man who had been cementing a camouflaged listening device over the lock fell on the apartment floor. His bent knees, upon which he had been resting, had buckled. I kicked him under the jaw as hard as I could. He bent up, and then rolled over and down on the floor, and then lay very still. His right hand fell open, and his laser pistol rolled out of it.

"James!" Genevieve cried.

"Quiet," I said, and then started to examine the man. He was connected with the Archbishop's staff in some manner; of that I was certain. Hidden in his habit were three other audio devices of various forms, a tape recorder, and a tiny television camera (two dimensional) that apparently could be hidden in a ventilation outlet.

I had kicked him too hard.

He was dead.

His neck was broken.

". . . perhaps we can all benefit from Christ's parable as told by Luke," the minister said as the priest began his rest through the layman's Homily. "That parable which concerns itself," the minister went on, "with a fig tree."

Twenty-two worshipers were in attendance.

"What is surprising about this particular parable," the minister said, "is Christ's choice of details. Well, to be really particular, the fig tree parable concerns God's patience with the Jewish nation; but why, of all things for illumination, a fig tree? Remember Adam and Eve and nudity? But let us get to the point.

"The story Christ related was about a man who at one time had a fig tree growing in his garden, but when that man came to look for figs there weren't any. Disgusted, for he had been waiting a good three years for fruit, the man told his gardener to cut the tree down, for it wasted space. But perhaps the gardener was a more patient man, for he answered: 'Master, don't touch it until I get a chance to dig around it and spread some manure. If it takes after that, fine. If not, then cut it down.'"

The minister smiled.

"This parable is really a story of much beauty," he said, "for in a few clear words it tells of many things: God's love in His creation, God's patience, and man's duty to his brothers in teaching the ways of our Lord, for . . ."

The minister started to bend backward oddly, grabbing the sides of the lectern.

". . . in each man," he went on, his knees buckling.

He was falling to the floor.

". . . the quality of his Creator can . . ."

The monks burst open the door of Gates's church.

". . . live."

The congregation shot up from the benches into a wave of laser and rapid submachine gun fire.

The doors surrounding the altar slammed open, the first man on the right was cut down, but three priests with weapons made it out to places of cover within the altar area, and the church's machine guns opened up.

The errant light of a spotlight, swinging on now extended wires from the ceiling, shone in the glazed, open eyes of a worshiper who half lay, half sat, on a bench, bloody and dead.

The priest of the service fell as the laser charred off his leg. Although the major vessels had been sealed, it began to bleed, yet he began to crawl forward to save the Host.

"So, my citizens," the new King said before the stereo cameras, "I am thus forced by the threat of war, in order that my authority be recognized as that of the highest, and that a cabinet be firmly established, to prematurely take the throne without blessings.

"Custom, and its duty, demand that we mourn for our late king thirty days before we allow a new government to be, and though we truly desire to obey that tradition, I cannot, I will not, succumb to those forces which resulted in my father's death. When peace is finally reassured—that will be the time when I shall lay down my crown for our Church's validification."

"We have petitioned the prince," Wayne said in a loud voice, "to allow us to cast aside this Church of Satan, and yet he refuses.

"We have demanded for the safety of his soul that he cast aside the teachings of an adulterated Bible, the lewd, evil teachings of the devil, and he refused us.

"And now, in his surroundings of lusts, dishonesties, and villainy, he dares to profane the spirit of our late King Gregory by prematurely claiming the throne without God's blessing."

The candle flame flickered.

"To so steal a hallowed crown," Wayne said in a dramatically quiet voice, "is to spit in the holy Face of God."

He picked up the candle and held it before his face. "Therefore," he said, "may he be denied the bosom of the Church, all rites of the Church, and eternal salvation. May he be excommunicated and dispatched on his eventual death to the most fiery bottom of bitter Hell, to suffer eternal damnation."

"They've taken the body away, love," I said. "He left no stain. Tomorrow, I shall fill out a report, and that shall be the end of it."

"James, he was going to kill you!"

"Yes," I said, "but it's murder still the same. What? Can't you understand? Am I . . . am I to capitalize on the flaws of my brother? Take advantage of them? Am I to make judgment on him? I have no power to do so; I have no right. I have killed him. Why did I kill him? Because he wanted to kill me. Could I have stopped him? Maybe. I took the convenient way out. May he sleep peacefully now. In Heaven."

She held two closed fingers over her mouth, staring at me.

"What difference does self-defense make? Heaven's the same to any man—there are no differences in perfection."

She put her arms around me, as I stood before her where she was seated on the couch.

"Doesn't life have any real deep meaning to you, Sir James? Is it all just a simple prelude?"

"Now," I said, "I am cold, Genevieve. Within me there is ice. A bitter ice."

She broke away.

"We are to die," I said. "Then why are we to live?"

"No man can be that way," she cried. Then softly: "Not you, at least. For in your eyes, Sir James, I see better things buried, only you won't let them come out."

"These better things," I said quickly. "They are your fantasy. Colored by a vile, unimaginable emotion that some label love; but I am certain it cannot exist."

"Ah, but there you are wrong." She laughed. "Perhaps in the past, Sir James, you were mistaken—the road is rough, but if two people combine into one and yet remain two, if two people come together, miracles can happen, my love. Miracles."

"I cannot believe in miracles," I said.

She placed her hand on the full-length zipper that ran up and down the length of her clothing. She stared at me. I looked down at her.

"Why must I be," I said to my hands, "so divided that the parts in me must clash within my naked skull, that my broken soul demands my death, and yet that one sweet part, that one dominating part, must say—love, James. Abandon all that seems important, for only love's important. That love, that impossible emotion, must be made possible because without love there is no meaning to this place, to this position, to this world, to this God."

Her hands started to lower the zipper downward, quickly.

"I am weak," I said.

And then I saw her body, and my mind became trapped within the beauty of it. But more than lust seemed to be there. Her eyes, that was what shocked me. Her naked, echoing eyes.

"Yes," I said. "I have loved you since my trial. I have not admitted it. Is that all you ask of me?"

"No, James," she said. "I ask nothing of you. I can only accept what you give me, and hope that you accept what I give you. There can be no debts."

"Then," I said, taking her hand and drawing her up close to me, "we shall not make any."

Military troops now arrived at Gates's church, armed with gases and anti-riot gear, but this was no riot—this was warfare.

The lieutenant in command was gunned down first.

There was a sergeant who took charge and ordered that

some rounds of gas be fired, and the church was soon filled with it, but as the sergeant turned a laser beam found its mark, and tore a foot-wide hole through his back and chest; his guts spilled out all over the corridor's floor.

Three of Gates's ministers swarmed out of the left door of the altar, submachine guns firing, through the gas clouds, and charged the monks stationed at the church's main entrance. The three died. They also knocked out the rapid-rapid fire machine gun and crew placed there.

A man was shot as he started to throw an anti-personnel grenade. He fell on the worshiper's body within the front pew. The grenade exploded there, spattering blood, bones, and tissue into the splinters of wood.

Fresh armed troops arrived, and together, fifty men all told, they rushed the monks from the outside with laser rifles, M/C 34's, and occasional knives. Eleven Republic men were shot down as they advanced. A scuffle ensued. Killer knives flashed in the gas clouds, and more men fell.

The one-legged priest with the Host crawled to the door on the altar's right, and expired in the arms of a man there who passed the Host to Gates, who then took it and protected it with his body.

The monks started to give up.

They were cut down by the soldiers, either laser burned, vaporized, or slit with a knife, and they began to drop like large insects to the slippery floor beneath them.

Gates told his men to cease fire.

The troops finished their jobs, and found they had thirty-one dead monks on their hands, and another twenty-nine bodies in the church.

The captain in charge of the troops swore loudly.

The priests and ministers of Gates's Church carefully walked out of their rooms behind the altar, guns ready, and stared at the troops outside the church, and the bodies in the pews.

The captain pointed to the bodies without saying a word.

Gates's ministers and priests put down their weapons, and then started to work.

The secretive stereovision cameras zoomed in for a tight close-up of the crown, and the upward motion of the new King's arms as the crown went up to a position above the new King's skull.

With one sharp puff, Wayne blew out the candle, and the wick began to smoke.

And then the hands came down in a soft motion until the crown was firmly in position on the skull.

Wayne smashed the smoking end of the candle into the altar, and part of the wax cracked and shattered, spilling on the floor.

"God save me," the King muttered.

"Go," Wayne told his audience. "This service is over."

A VU meter kicked; then the needle settled on its peg.

# XV

There was a ground squirrel, asleep.

He was all wrapped up, for the air here was cold at night; the heat of the sun had radiated off into the clear night.

The animal's breath was slow and regular and shallow in character.

His brownish fur had a more sandy tinge than his forefathers had had.

There was a new sensation.

The ground squirrel opened one slightly furred eye.

And now there was a momentary silence in the burrow's air.

The insects had stopped, and there was only the wind for company.

Up went the other eye, and up went the squirrel's ears from beneath his warm, rather comfortable tail. Up went his respiration. Up went the rate of his breath.

Night time.

That one not too near.

The ground was vibrating, a very soft yet not relaxing vibration, for the squirrel was smart enough to know not to trust a vibrating earth.

Bits of unhinged dirt began to silently swing from the ceiling of the burrow on root threads.

Alarmed, the ground squirrel came to attention, quivered, and sniffed the air. He was a squirrel rather reluctant to instant commitment.

From the south to south-southwest?

With a blurred chatter, the ground squirrel spewed out of his emergency exit tunnel which led away from the south at a right angle to the east where, he remembered, a fallen wall and a pile of concrete stone lay on the surface.

Under the clear sky they came. The moonlight was not yet there. It was starlight that gleamed off the polished sides of their machinery. There were helmeted, dull-colored, suited men silent behind the thick glass windshields. Shadows of aircraft were in the distance, now approaching the squirrel, screaming, passing, and leaving.

Man-made, the ground squirrel observed.

". . . and troop carriers, my lord," he said. "All of it pretty massive stuff, heavily powered—I'd say maybe two thousand men."

"Are you certain of that figure?" I asked.

At seventy miles per hour they came. Floating seventeen inches off the earth on their gravitation fields, they were virtually inertialess craft, and they left a subsonic impression of their sound on the earth.

Heavy tanks.

Light tanks with higher capabilities of speed and maneuverability.

All running.

All scattered as far as the ground squirrel could see into the night, and to him they were mysterious shapes in that night where a moon was needed.

"Are you certain of identification?" the King said.

"I have no doubt, your highness," the major replied. "I've got a shot-up aircraft to prove it, sir, and those were Chicago model craft that did it."

Disgusted, the ground squirrel shook, for it was cold. And he felt cheated. His thoughts on the subject were easily detected, as he kicked a small stone with his paw at the advancing ranks. Men, messing around again, he thought. What waste.

". . . but only after I had made four passes over them," the major explained. "And I got everything back." He smiled.

"And you got everything back," the King repeated. "But now they know! They know we're waiting for them. Before . . . perhaps they thought we had no suspicions after their attack on our aircraft, and the Republic itself, but now in their act they have been observed."

"It makes no difference," I said, leaning on the mantel, sipping my wine.

"It makes a world of difference," the King said, leaning on the arm of his chair.

"Surely you realize, my lord, that it's stupid to pit men against our nuclear weaponry."

He looked up at me with a frown.

"We have a group of planes ready, my lord. We converted ten warheads from our ICBM supply to be dropped."

"We are to bomb them?" the King asked softly.

"At the proper moment."

"Which is?"

"When they start to group together for the attack. Most of the battle will be fought in the skies. We will try to defeat their air force so that the bombs can be dropped."

"But that will decimate their ground forces."

I set the remains of my wine down on the mantel.

"Thus is our intention, and our guarantee of peace."

. . . Christ died to save us from damnation, he said. Can't you understand what I speak?

The King's face twitched.

. . . it was a dream a dream a dream from heaven, sir, that we perform, perform . . .

The King ordered that the major leave.

. . . the darkness, it will close over you, my lord . . .
. . . you are mistaken, mistaken. I cannot be denied . . .

"Pour me some wine, James," the King said softly.

"Certainly."

The King's hand shook as he held the glass in which I poured the burgundy. I looked at his eyes, but they were focused on the glass and not mine.

. . . there is but one church, my lord; God's church, and no other. It's stated so in God's book. Frank advice, my lord: do not comply with sinners who have profaned God's words. Renounce your decision. We ask only for unity to be restored. Bring peace to your subjects. God wants to extend this final grace to you . . .

"Now we must wait for the enemy to group, my lord," I said.

"Yes," the King replied. "Three hours into the day, and we must wait."

. . . I offer you salvation. I offer you the grace of God at the risk of my own life . . .

"Patience can win wars," I said.
"If patience fought one," the King replied.

. . . do not deny God . . .

Now a silence came to us. The King was seated in his chair before his fire, ten feet away from it, and though I stopped looking at him, though I lost my sight within the artificial flame, my back could feel his presence with me here.

A statue's presence.

Lifeless, yet possessed with life, an irony in concrete-stone, or marble.

"I see him in the flames, there, James."

"See who, Robert?"

"Just a face. Haven't you ever seen faces in a fire, James?"

"In a real fire, yes, but not in one of these."

"All it takes is imagination, James."

"With imagination, we'd all be kings."

"The cremation, James."

"Sir?"

"Fire," the King said, and then he laughed.

"Sir?" I said.

"For everything shoved down the Big Fall, James, everything gets heated in the process. It all gets burned by that little artificial sun at the bottom of the Fall. The descent is slowed until it seems motionless, or it may be accelerated until it seems a streak of light to the impossible eye. Heated, everything is well broken up before ever kissing that magnetically bonded sun. Everything enters it for a final purification for the transfer to a virgin state. And it's all guided by man and his dollar and his gravitation so the reaction's efficient, cheap, and controlled—the rot must wait and be metered in at the proper moment."

He looked at the shaking wine in his trembling hand.

"How strange I feel," he said in a disgusted manner.

"Are you ill, my lord?"

"No," he said after a long moment. "No, for as with everything, it all comes to a point within my imperfect mind. I feel, I feel as if time, James, has gathered itself up and now has taken residence within my brain. My head's a fulcrum for it."

"It's the hour, Robert," I said. "It is late. The enemy . . ."

"My kingdom is tearing itself apart, James!" the King cried, rising from his chair, his unnoticed wine spilling on the floor. "Can't you feel the firmament ripping? Those lines of

control? Order? We have to use five hundred troops to keep
order. We shouldn't need any. Seventy-two dead, now. Is
one too many? You know that answer. Our jails are packed
with teeming rebels.

"My soul," he gasped. He collapsed back into his chair.
"My soul's found its imperfection."

A servant opened the door of the King's chambers.

"You're confused, Robert," I said, gripping his shoulders.
"We have no civil war. Man, the rebels are all in Wayne's
pay, our intelligence confirms that, and Wayne is nowhere to
be found. Some say he's even left for Chicago to lead their
army. Sir, the population doesn't support the rebellion, very
little, if any, support is given. Can't you understand? They've
tired of their whores. To view this riot as a threat to your
throne, why, that's stupidity."

"We are all stupid," the King said.

"But we're men," I said.

"The throne's defective, James," he said softly.

"My lord?"

"James," he said, taking away my hands and rising. "Don't
you see, James? The King's only half there. The rest of him is
dead."

"But, Robert!"

He turned away and walked to the open door where the
generals would be gathering; he stood at it and shook his
head. "And the prince," he said. "He lacks the other half,
too."

Then, he started to go, but stopped before the first step
and looked at me for a long while.

"There shall be no nuclear weapons," he said finally.

# XVI

"The time's coming up on us! Realize that! Observe that! Taste it, smell it, see it, and eat it! Time, time, necessary time! I am on call. I am waiting. They know not where I am or what I do, but they have the means to call me on my wrist here."

"Come anyway," she said.

"Where? Darling, darling, need I say more screams? We may be interrupted at any moment, our timing may be thrown ajar; what sense is commencement?"

"Come with me, Sir James."

"That I desire to go should be evident, but no, dear love, let's stay here in our crowd and surround ourselves with illusion."

"What should be important to us, James?" she said softly. "That I'm a woman and you're a man? That's known. So we are disturbed. Must the importance of lives be that which we do well together, not the intention? What do you make your love out of? Must all the earthy things smell of perfection at all times? Is God that little human in composition?"

Her eyes began to gather moisture as her body began to shake.

I looked at my hands. Perspective, was the word I said.

"My dear Sir James," she cried softly. "Come with me."

"No," I replied just as softly. "Please not tonight. All other nights, yes, but tonight . . ."

"Let's not stay here alone, James."

"I . . ."

The bed.

"I don't understand," she said.

"I never asked you for it," I said. "Tonight, it's no solution."

She was silent as I opened my eyes and stared at her, she sitting on the bed holding the bed clothes up to her quiet, white neck, and her hair was caught in the process of falling around that neck. The fasteners of my uniform were yet to be touched.

"Don't be upset or hurt or insulted," I tried to comfort. "Oh, beautiful, beautiful, I'm in need of a different assurance tonight. Assurance of the same sweetness, but no, please no, not this method. Leave it to a happier time where it can live in a better light. Don't cry. Love of your soul tonight, oh yes —that I have and promise to keep worthy of. But for this formidable, firm commitment of yourself tonight, I desire you . . . but the hour's too darkish and cold. This body's too cold. And the atmosphere has yet to experience a temperature, save neutrality."

"What has struck you, Sir James?" she said, the weeping in her voice.

"Life . . . it is life that struck me."

"So much as to make you wear this mood?"

"I am diseased with life."

She was crying so carefully.

"And no needle can cure me," I went on. "The rot has got to the advanced stage where I can smell it firmly; no, it has thrust its stink into my nose. I am infected—my dreams are realities! The rot will come to take me in my nakedness."

"Oh, that's not so!"

"And no need now for burial! Or the Big Fall! Oh, look at me: the genius living a damned lie! And what's more, my dear doctor: deliberately. And why? Here's the trivial: to promote the infection—to live! Now weep, my love, if that will do you good, but really—it is all hypocrisy, and nothing higher or more."

"Oh, quiet! Quiet!"

"I knew of this system of underground cities before they dispatched me on my interstellar mission. They told me that they hoped they would never be used. Perhaps they knew that the war would come. The cities were supposed to continue a way of life that had failed when the rest had been burned away. That, it did not . . . but God . . . God . . . God, look what replaced it! A paradox of trite myth! A confusion of order! An abridgment of history spat about and misused! A progression of time? Archbishops as whoremasters, the individual preprogrammed, lies as replacement for truth, and all for what?"

There was a movement on the bed where I now sat facing away. I felt her naked breasts form themselves against my back, her body's warmth, and then the soft press of her lips against my neck.

"I will not fit here," I said quietly.
"We will not fit here," she said.
"Marry me."
"Why?"
"Why not?"


YELLOW
YELLOW
YELLOW


I raised my right wrist away from her hand and glanced at the metallic device strapped there in artificial leather.

YELLOW

Then, softly, I broke free of her, got up from the bed, and walked out into the living room of my apartment.

YELLOW

At the door, I heard her voice again before I started to open it.

YELLOW

"When?" she said.


". . . by for Condition Red," Henderson was saying as I entered Defense Command, and the elevator doors closed behind me.
"Deployment of troops as per orders completed," came a rushed voice from a speaker somewhere.

curious little bits of motion were in the process of their creations, stimulated by the proper electrical commands

a*
m*a*n* p*a*s*s*e*d* b*y*
w*i*t*h aseriesofcodeorderbooks
that *h*e*l*d *t*h*e *i*n*v*a*s*i*o*n
*c*o*n*t*i*n*g*e*n*c*y
*p*l*a*n*s
lightpensflashed


"Strange," I said.
"What's strange?" the general asked, looking up from a special electronic table that had been recently installed on which, photonically plotted, were the mechanized elements of both sides.

"This environment," I said.

*thummm*

A man, a sergeant technician by rank, caught my eye.

"That's the shock springs, sir," he said. "We've been firing anti-personnel missiles on the surface—so's the enemy. They hit the ground, and our blast system catches the vibrations."

"That's a soft sound."

"It's probably not as pleasant on Level one, sir."

"Condition Red," Henderson said.

RED
RED
RED

"Tone down that alarm!" I cried. "For God's sake, you'll wake up the spirits of Hell!"

The general gave a slight laugh at this.

RED
RED
RED

"Sir Defense Minister," Henderson said calmly. "If you'll observe with me . . ."

I leaned over his electronic table.

"Sir," he began. "From what we can detect, the enemy has grouped itself into two forces."

"Just perfect for nuclear attack," I muttered.

"Yes," Henderson crisply replied. "From our GEA, Ground Energies Analysis, we figure each group at roughly five hundred attack vehicles each. One group is attacking from due west and, for reasons I shall state later, I believe this is in order to create a diversion. Group two appears to be circulating for an attack from the northeast."

"And try to knock out system four on the way, eh?"

"Precisely," Henderson said. "And that's a good plan, too. Yet, other than a zone defense, I haven't committed my troops to disperse group two."

"Why?"

Henderson looked at my eyes. "The decoy plot is obvious —draw us out to the west, knock out our missiles, wreck our main force, and attack a weak north. My question is this: why would the Defense Computer indicate two flight paths for their anti-personnel missiles? Normally, it should be only one."

"What are the flight plans?"

"One from the west, the other indicating a liftoff in the ruins of Detroit."

"What has air recon to say?"

"There's the difficulty: Enemy air units are engaged with us one hundred miles to the southeast—we're holding them back, but they're Chicago based. We've got too few planes to run a decent recon over Detroit."

I tapped the electronic desk with my fingertips.

"As for satellite coverage, someone knocked us out of orbit. The rocketry could be launched from mobile emplacements within the Tri-Scann coverage the city's ruins provide, set to fly low to be lost in the ground haze. Then they might ascend in the west, as one would normally expect for emplacements located in the west. A waste of fuel, yes, but again, it could be another attempt to draw us west."

"Brilliant," I said. "But unproven. What confirmation do you really have?"

"Only that Tri-Scann indicates some sort of heavy magnetic jamming in the Detroit area."

"Dammit!" I said, pounding the table.

"Yet," Henderson said, "I didn't know Tri-Scann could be effectively jammed like that."

"It's an electronic device like any other," I said irritably. "Why can't one mess it up?"

"Or make it perform tricks," Henderson whispered. "It could very well be that we're underestimating them, that we may have a three-pronged attack, or a two-pronged attack, or perhaps one."

"They've got to show their hand," I said softly.

"Sir," Henderson cried. "They are!"

"How can they fake gravity expenditures?"

"True, our GEA is based fundamentally on pickup of the enemy's gravitational fields, but what if they could use shielded projection, fired against the ground so that one machine could decoy a hundred?"

"A gravitation gun? The expenditures of power necessary, by God, they'd have to have a damn large, slow machine to do it with. Ten thousand tons of machine."

"Look at the ground speed of the two attack groups. Thirty-one miles per hour for one, twenty-nine for the other. That's pretty slow."

I looked at Henderson.

Henderson smiled at me.

When I looked up from the electronic desk again, Henderson was gone, replaced by ventilator air. He was at the Command Station in the center of Defense Command, standing by the seated duty officer, and he was speaking into his microphone.

"Will they be loyal?"

"They must, or they shall die on the surface without provisions as all sinners should die. They shall die of the sickness."

"What about the King?"

In the shadow caused by the casual lighting of the Level 14 main ventilation shaft, only Wayne's eyes could be seen.

"The Lord," he said, "has promised me that Satan shall claim him tonight."

"And so it must be," said a bishop.

"You all know the plans," Wayne went on. "Father Galbreth shall be our leader tonight since Father Reginwald is now in the hands of the Devil. This purification, need I say it, is most necessary."

"I still say we're taking all the risks," said the only priest of the five.

"But it's necessary," another bishop countered.

"Is it?" the priest said. "The King hasn't appointed a successor; I'm certain that if he's to die tonight our divine father will be asked to take over the government; he must for our salvation. This additional blood . . . it sickens me with its unnecessity."

"It's God's *will!*" Wayne screamed. "For whereas what you say seems true, and indeed it may smell of reason, now's not the time for it. God's purification must continue; we must cast Satan out! We must burn off those who are leading us to damnation with their tolerance of the rebel Gates, and we need the insurance of the complete control of the Republic in order to cure the blind!"

"Thus we are committed!" the first bishop said.

"We pledge our lives as our Lord Jesus pledged His," echoed another.

"Amen," chanted the group.

. . . the captain. He sat in his chair under the leaded glass observation bubble, the engines of his tank whining under him, the air flowing past his sweat-lined mouth and up into his helmet, slightly cooling his wet hair.

In formation they ran, undetected by the enemy as the enemy fired rockets in a barrage around the parameter of the Republic. As a ploy, a small group of light tanks ran off to meet the decoy weaponry.

No moon.

No moon.

No moon, the captain thought.

The sounds of the explosions of war would reach his and his companion's ears, but they were far from his tank yet; they seemed far away. It was like any other training mission, rushing over the ground at eighty miles per hour with all running lights out, maximum radio silence—the instructor standing on the platform behind the seat.

No planes of any kind in the night's air.

They were fighting elsewhere.

The King.

The King.

The King.

"He's not in his quarters, sir," he said.

I looked at Henderson. I looked back at the soldier. I looked at the desk and saw that our troops were moving in formation perfectly, and that contact was only minutes away now. I looked at the steam that was rising from my coffee.

"Not again," I muttered. "Where could he be?"

"Not in safety," the soldier said.

"What?"

"There's been a rumor, sir," the soldier said, "that the night before yesterday, the King had a visit from the Archbishop."

"Wayne? Where?"

"In the King's quarters, sir."

WILL THAT BE ALL, SIR?
WILL THAT BE ALL, SIR?

"Continue the search," I cried. "Find him! Goddamn it, find him! For the love of Jesus, find him! For the love of God!"

an explosion

"Henderson! Down!"

The emergency exit hatch glared up in a bright light, then fell off into the rest of Level 15—to the outside of Defense Command.

Somebody had hit the alarm.

The elevator doors slammed open, and out ran twelve

guards, two of whom were hit by the fire that thrust through the open hatchway, and were blown apart by the M/C laser beams.

"Auxiliaries!" Henderson shouted. "Switch to auxiliary command, all stations. Somebody, short that main power board!"

Two men on watch were killed performing the latter task.

"They dare not use anything explosive," I cried at Henderson, "that is, if they want to take Defense Command intact."

Three men in monk's robes rushed screaming toward us.

A lieutenant fired. A captain fired. Other safeties were slammed off.

A man, on whose side the identification was not clear, was caught in a cross fire; then there was nothing but bits of him over the floor.

Now they opened up with the hard weaponry. Explosive bullets began to burst over the walls. A PCM shattered in a riot of electrons.

"Dammit."

"Sir?"

"Just a fragment," I said. "Not too deep."

Outside explosions.

The gunfire stopped through the hatch frame.

"Reinforcements," said a lieutenant, peering over a dead monk's body which lay on the floor against the platform of the Command Station. "Attacking from the rear."

I got up.

Henderson pulled himself up too.

There wasn't too much blood coming from the spot where the bottom of my rib cage was located; what little there was had a color darkish to the eye.

"Get medical aid down here," I said. I saw then that Henderson had taken a wound too, in the right arm, and it was bleeding swiftly.

"Sir?" he said.

"Take care of that arm," I said, stepping over a dead bishop.

"It was Wayne, sir," the colonel said on the other side.

"I know," I said, holding my side and peering through the thick smoke in the corridors that the ventilators had yet to suck away.

"We got him. He's wounded, but alive. Do you wish to speak to him?"

"No," I told him. "Throw him in military jail. I know what he will say."

"Sir?"

"That the King is dead. Or soon will be. Unless . . ."

"Unless what, sir?"

"Unless we contain that death."

The Colonel became silent.

"Aren't you tired of it all? Senseless murders? Who's in charge here? And does it matter?"

"Sir!"

"Henderson?"

I turned and saw him through the broken hatchway; I saw him holding his bleeding arm with the blood caked about his fingers.

"We've located the King, sir!"

"The King? Where?"

"Attack Force A, Tank five-seventy-two, heavy . . ."

Back through the hatch to the elevator.

I ran.

# XVII

There was a battle.

It was really an orgy.

Not much of an orgy.

There were tanks and missile carriers, some men without tanks in radiation suits and hand equipment. These were the forces of a series of technologies at play with themselves.

They were an admirable enemy to each other.

Steel filled the dawn's air, the ascent of the sun gleamed off the fresh breaks of it, and flame challenged that sun.

Other trite sayings.

Men flew, at least for a little distance, pushed up by detonation, with their bodies held together more by the strength of their equipment than by the strength of their flesh.

I ran.

In a radiation suit, and then in an unarmed surface transport pulling a grand speed of forty-five miles per hour—a small, two-man craft whose range was no more than two hundred miles. It had no nuclear reactor to supply the power of propulsion—it used batteries.

A shortage of oil.

When I arrived at what appeared to be the battlefield, I landed the craft—that is, I let it settle twelve inches to the earth. I got out and ran for cover. But the enemy was in retreat now, and the wreckage about was beginning to turn dull.

Like a faded dream.

faded dream
faded dream

The King rested against the side of a heavy tank that had suffered a direct hit by missile, the tank was numbered 572, and the King wore no helmet, for his suit had been ripped open.

The King was half there.

For whereas his face was still there intact, and the bulk of his body was there, his right side was almost missing—there was no arm and leg, and there was a lot of spilled blood.

Like a toy, he was dead.

There was an army sergeant nearby who was still very much alive, although he had taken off his suit to effectively bind his wound with gauze and medicines—that is, the stump of his left leg. Since his suit no longer held air, it made no big difference whether or not he wore it.

I bent over him.

He was holding a tight tourniquet about the stump, and he was staring off somewhere beyond me.

A tiny, two-inch speaker was activated in the chest pack of my suit.

"Hello," I said.

"Hello."

"What happened?"

"We were hit."

"Were you in the same tank as the King?"

"Yes."

"What happened to him?"

"He saved me from the inside."

"But he's blown apart."

"No, he was hit after the inside exploded. You must understand. When the tank was first hit, I lost it in the gunnery B seat. He cut my belts and pulled me out. He threw this bandage on me. We got here just as the anti-personnel ammo went; the tank's armor somehow held. He told me to keep the bandage tight, he did. Then he went up on the tank to see if any of the remaining bastards survived. He got cut off by a heavy laser beam. I watched it all."

Quietly, I hit the medic alarm on my suit's radio.

"If they get me quick," the soldier said, "before I breathe too much of this stuff in, I'll be OK, won't I?"

"Sure," I said. "Did the King have anything else to say?"

. . . keep my people alive. Oh God, keep my people alive. I know we're as ignorant as hell, as stupid as the lowest form of life and incapable of wisdom, but, dear God, keep my people alive and free to themselves . . .

The private turning of the eyes to me . . .

"Patience," he said. "The King told me that what we need is patience for each other. When that's coupled with the love all men possess for each other, that's the secret of Heaven."

The earth.

The earth.

A hand brushed the side of my leg. I looked down and saw the sergeant leaning over to give me something that hung from a silver chain.

"Here, sir," he said. "Perhaps you can make more use of this thing the King gave me than I can."